Superstitions: Unraveling the Threads of Belief

Porsha Garrett

I would like to dedicate this book to my dad, who is a very superstitious old man. Yet a wise one, who always told me about every single one. And to my boys Jayden & Karter who made me love the number 13 as one was born on that day, and the other in room 13 on the 13th hour.

I love you guys

Prologue

In a world brimming with mysteries, where the line between fact and fiction blurs, there exists a tapestry of beliefs woven into the fabric of human existence. Superstitions, they are called, passed down through generations, whispered in hushed tones, and embraced with both skepticism and reverence. These tales, rooted in ancient folklore and steeped in the human psyche, have found a way to transcend time, capturing our imaginations and shaping our cultural landscape.

Come, dear reader, and embark on a journey through the rich tapestry of superstitions, where we shall unravel the stories behind the 20 most popular beliefs. Prepare to be enchanted, as we traverse the realms of myth and legend, uncovering the origins and backstories that have given rise to these enduring superstitions. But remember, dear reader, that the following accounts are works of fiction, designed to entertain and delight. So, sit back, relax, and let your mind wander into the realm of the unknown.

Walking Under a Ladder

"This is considered bad luck. It's thought to originate from the idea that ladders create a triangle with the ground"

THE CURSED LADDER

Eric had always been a superstitious man, a trait inherited from his grandmother who spent her twilight years reading tarot cards and whispering incantations under her breath. He avoided black cats, was careful not to break mirrors, and never, ever walked under ladders. Until one day, he did.

On a windy afternoon, Eric was walking home from the local bookstore, his bag filled with the latest horror novels. As he turned the corner onto his street, he noticed a ladder leaning against the building. Some window washers were working above, their suds and buckets hanging precariously overhead. Distracted by his phone, he stepped under the ladder without a second thought.

The moment he crossed beneath it, a shiver ran down his spine as if he'd just stepped over a grave. He looked back at the ladder, feeling a sudden unease creeping into his mind. He brushed it off as a silly superstition and walked on. But that night, the nightmares began.

Eric found himself in a world that mirrored his own, but distorted in a horrific way. His house was dilapidated, the streets outside were deserted, and the sky was a sickly shade of green. Shadows moved without their owners, and whispers echoed from nowhere. He would wake up in a cold sweat, the images so vivid he could still smell the rot and decay.

The dreams persisted, getting worse each night. He began to see figures in the corner of his vision during the day, shadows that flitted away when he turned to look. His house, once a sanctuary, now echoed with strange noises at night. He heard whispers in the silence, always too soft to comprehend but chilling to the bone.

One day, as he walked past the mirror in his hallway, he froze. His reflection stood independent, grinning back at him with an unnatural, sinister smile. His heart pounded in his chest as his reflection raised a hand, gesturing him closer. Panicked, he smashed the mirror, shards of glass scattering like diamonds on the floor. But even in the shards, his reflection continued to grin back.

Overwhelmed with terror, Eric sought help. He went to psychologists, priests, even a local paranormal investigator, but none could provide an answer. The nightmares, the apparitions, his rebellious reflection - all were dismissed as figments of an overactive imagination, stress, or lack of sleep.

Desperate, he visited his grandmother's old friend, a woman named Agnes who was known in the town as a white witch. As he poured out his story, Agnes listened, her eyes narrowing.

"You walked under a ladder, you said?" she asked, her voice barely above a whisper.

"Yes, but that's just a superstition, isn't it?" Eric replied, a glimmer of hope sparking in his eyes.

Agnes shook her head, "Some superstitions, child, are warnings. You opened a door, Eric, to a world that should've remained closed."

With Agnes's help, Eric devised a plan to close the portal. According to her instructions, he needed to pass under the same ladder again, but this time in his nightmare. She gave him a talisman, a small amulet filled with herbs and inscribed with ancient symbols, to protect him from the malevolent entities in that other dimension.

That night, Eric went to sleep holding the talisman, the scent of Agnes's protective herbs filling his nostrils. He found himself back in the nightmarish world, the sickly green sky looming above. His heart pounded as he made his way through the deserted streets, following the path he took on that fateful afternoon.

The ladder was there, just as it was in his reality. It stood ominously against the crumbling building, a beacon in the dismal landscape. He could feel an intense evil radiating from it, a dark vortex that threatened to swallow him whole. But he had to do this. He had to close the portal.

As he stepped towards the ladder, an inhuman howl filled the air. From the shadows, grotesque figures emerged, their eyes glowing with malice. They advanced towards him, their forms flickering like shadows dancing in candlelight.

His heart raced, his body screamed to run, but he stood his ground. He clutched the amulet tightly, the sharp edges digging into his palm. As the entities got closer, he could hear their whispers growing louder, a cacophony of voices that drowned everything else.

Just as they were about to reach him, Eric stepped under the ladder. A blinding light erupted from the amulet, enveloping him in a protective glow. The entities shrieked as they were thrown back, their forms disintegrating in the light.

He felt a strong pull, as if he was being sucked into a vortex. He closed his eyes, the talisman's light burning against his eyelids. Then, suddenly, he was falling.

Eric woke up with a start, his bed sheets drenched in sweat. His heart was pounding, but the chilling dread was gone. He looked around, half expecting to see the distorted reality of his nightmares. But he was in his room, the familiar surroundings bathed in the soft glow of the morning sun.

Days turned into weeks, and the nightmares didn't return. His reflection was back to normal, mirroring his actions like it should. The whispers were gone, and his house was once again a sanctuary, filled with peace and quiet.

Walking past the building one day, he noticed the ladder still leaning against it. He felt a shiver run down his spine, but this time, it was not out of fear. It was a chilling reminder of the ordeal he had faced, a haunting memory of the door he had opened and thankfully managed to close.

And from that day forward, Eric made sure to give ladders a wide berth, his grandmother's old superstitions firmly embedded in his mind. After all, some superstitions might just be warnings from the past, meant to keep us safe from the unseen horrors that lurk in the shadows.

Now let's break down this superstition of walking under a ladder:

The superstition about walking under a ladder has roots in various cultures and periods of history, reflecting common beliefs about spiritual and physical safety. While many people today might dismiss it as a harmless tradition or an eccentric quirk, it can be traced back to ancient civilizations and religious beliefs.

1. Ancient Egypt:
The Egyptians considered the triangle a sacred symbol. Since a ladder leaning against a wall forms a triangle with the ground, walking

under it was seen as desecrating the sacred shape. The Egyptians were known for their rigorous rites and ceremonies, and breaking these rules was considered a bad omen.

2. Christianity:

The superstition has also been linked to Christianity, as you mentioned in your question. The ladder against a wall forms a triangle, which could be interpreted as a representation of the Holy Trinity (Father, Son, and Holy Spirit). Walking under the ladder, then, might be seen as breaking or disrespecting the Trinity, a blasphemous act which would be bound to attract bad luck.

3. Medieval Europe:

In medieval times, ladders were associated with executions. A ladder was often leaned against the gallows where people were hanged. To walk under such a ladder was considered a grim foreshadowing of one's own death by hanging, hence it was seen as an act inviting bad luck.

4. Physical Safety:

On a more pragmatic level, walking under a ladder is a safety hazard. Workers may drop tools or materials from above, and the ladder itself could lose balance and fall. This practical reason could have strengthened the superstition over time.

Like many superstitions, the belief about walking under a ladder is a blend of cultural, religious, and practical considerations. It's a way for societies to express their respect for the unknown, their religious beliefs, and their concern for safety. Today, even if people don't believe in the spiritual consequences, they might still avoid walking under ladders simply because they've been taught that it's an unsafe act.

Breaking a Mirror

"It's often said that breaking a mirror brings seven years of bad luck."

THE VENGEFUL MIRROR

Allysa was never one to believe in superstitions. She scoffed at the idea of black cats bringing bad luck and walked under ladders without a care in the world. But one fateful day, her skepticism would be shattered, just like the mirror she broke.

It happened in her grandmother's old attic. Allysa was sorting through dusty boxes, searching for a particular family heirloom. In her haste, she accidentally knocked over a small table, sending a large antique mirror crashing to the floor. The sound of shattering glass filled the air, and Allysa's heart skipped a beat.

She stood frozen in disbelief, staring at her reflection in the broken mirror. But something was off. Her reflection was... different. It moved independently, its movements disjointed and unnatural. It grinned at her, revealing rows of sharp, jagged teeth. A chill ran down Allysa's spine as she realized she was witnessing her own reflection behaving strangely.

Days turned into nights, and the strangeness continued. Allysa's reflection would mimic her actions with a malicious twist. It would laugh when she cried, sneer when she smiled, and display a twisted joy in her moments of pain. Allysa tried to ignore it at first, chalking it up to her imagination playing tricks on her. But as the days wore on and the reflection's actions grew more malevolent, she knew she had to confront the truth.

Unable to bear the torment any longer, Allysa delved into the mystery of the broken mirror. She researched ancient folklore and consulted with paranormal experts. The more she dug, the clearer it became that the mirror held a vengeful spirit trapped within its shattered fragments. Legend spoke of a malevolent entity that preyed on those who dared to break mirrors, seeking revenge for its own shattered existence.

Armed with this knowledge, Allysa embarked on a dangerous quest to free herself from the spirit's grip. She gathered the broken mirror fragments, carefully placing them on a table. Her hands trembled as she lit candles around the room, casting an eerie glow on the shards. She took a deep breath and chanted an incantation she had discovered in her research.

As the words left her lips, the room grew cold. The air crackled with an otherworldly energy, and a mist began to swirl around the mirror fragments. Allysa watched in awe as the mist condensed, taking the form of a shadowy figure. The vengeful spirit had materialized before her.

The spirit's eyes blazed with rage, its voice filled with a haunting echo. It revealed the pain and suffering it had endured, trapped within the mirror for centuries. The broken shards were its only connection to the physical world, and it resented those who had shattered its vessel.

Allysa spoke with empathy, acknowledging the spirit's anguish. She pleaded for forgiveness, vowing to find a way to set it free. The spirit's wrath softened, and a flicker of hope appeared in its eyes. It revealed a ritual that could release its grip on Allysa's reflection, allowing both of them to find peace.

Allysa followed the spirit's instructions meticulously. She performed the ritual, a complex dance of light and shadow, as the spirit watched carefully. The room filled with an ethereal glow, and the mirror fragments trembled. And then, in a burst of blinding light, the spirit disappeared, its presence released from the shattered mirror.

Allysa stood in the aftermath of the ritual, the broken mirror fragments now motionless and devoid of any supernatural presence. She felt a weight lifted from her shoulders, a sense of relief washing over her. The torment of her reflection's twisted actions had ceased.

Days turned into weeks, and Allysa's life returned to normal. Her reflection once again mirrored her movements without any hint of malice or distortion. The memory of the vengeful spirit trapped within the shattered mirror lingered, a reminder of the dangers lurking within the realms of superstition.

Allysa became more cautious, more respectful of the old beliefs and superstitions. She avoided breaking mirrors, crossed her fingers for good luck, and took care not to step on cracks in the sidewalk. She had witnessed firsthand the power that lay beneath the surface of these seemingly innocuous practices.

But the ordeal had left its mark on Allysa. She couldn't help but feel a lingering unease whenever she looked into a mirror, a faint echo of the malevolence she had once encountered. She knew that some spirits never truly vanished and that she would always carry the memory of the vengeful entity within her.

As time passed, Allysa found solace in sharing her story with others. She became an advocate for understanding the supernatural forces that exist alongside our own reality. She dedicated herself to researching ancient artifacts, haunted objects, and the stories of those who had encountered the otherworldly.

In her quest for knowledge, Allysa discovered a way to seal away malevolent spirits permanently, preventing them from wreaking havoc on unsuspecting souls. She worked with paranormal experts and mediums, honing her skills in the ancient arts of protection and banishment.

Armed with her newfound expertise, Allysa traveled far and wide, helping those tormented by supernatural entities. She became a beacon of hope for those trapped in the clutches of the paranormal, offering guidance, support, and a means to find peace.

And as she faced each new challenge, Allysa carried the memory of the vengeful spirit trapped within the shattered mirror. It served as a constant reminder of the thin veil that separates our world from the realms of darkness and the importance of respecting the ancient superstitions that hold ancient wisdom.

For Allysa, the shattered mirror had become a catalyst for a greater purpose, transforming her into a guardian of the supernatural, a protector of those haunted by the unseen. And as she ventured forth, she knew that her encounters with the vengeful spirit had shaped her destiny, guiding her towards a path of understanding, compassion, and the pursuit of balance between the living and the spirit world.

Now let's break down this superstition of breaking a mirror:

The superstition about breaking a mirror and subsequently experiencing seven years of bad luck has a rich history that spans various cultures, but it's most often traced back to the ancient Romans. Here's a more detailed explanation:

1. Ancient Romans:
The Romans believed that life renewed itself every seven years, and that damaging a mirror

could damage one's soul for that period. They created mirrors by backing plates of metal with lead, and they thought that these mirrors could capture and hold part of the user's soul when they looked into it. So, if a mirror was broken, it would mean that the captured part of the soul was damaged too. The soul, they believed, wouldn't fully recover until the next seven-year cycle had passed.

2. Greek Mythology:

There's also a link to Greek mythology. It's said that Narcissus, a character known for his extraordinary beauty, fell in love with his reflection in a pool of water, not realizing it was merely an image. Unable to leave the allure of his image, Narcissus lost his will to live and stared at his reflection until he died. Thus, mirrors in ancient Greece were considered as objects of dangerous vanity that could lead to devastation.

3. Jewish Tradition:

In Jewish mourning tradition, mirrors in a house of mourning are often covered for the seven-day mourning period (called "sitting shiva"). This is done to de-emphasize personal vanity and outward appearances during a time of grief. Although not directly related to the superstition about breaking mirrors, it shows a cultural instance where mirrors are associated with spiritual and emotional implications.

4. Victorian England:
In 19th century England, it was believed that a mirror reflected not only a person's image but also their health and well-being. So, breaking a mirror would negatively affect the health of the person whose reflection it last held.

Like most superstitions, the belief about breaking mirrors combines cultural, spiritual, and historical elements. It's a way for societies to express their fears about the unknown and the potentially harmful consequences of everyday actions. Even today, many people may feel a moment of unease when a mirror breaks, even if they don't believe in the superstition.

Black Cats

"In some cultures, black cats are considered bad luck, especially if one crosses your path."

CURSE OF THE BLACK CAT

In the small town of Ravenswood, a sense of foreboding hung in the air. Superstitions ran deep, and none were more feared than the presence of a black cat. For generations, the townsfolk believed that encountering one would bring misfortune and tragedy. But what they didn't know was that their fears were about to become a chilling reality.

It began with whispers, tales of strange occurrences that seemed to follow the path of a particular black cat. People spoke of accidents, sudden illnesses, and unexplained deaths—all seemingly linked to this mysterious feline. Fear gripped the hearts of the townsfolk as more and more sinister incidents unfolded.

The residents of Ravenswood couldn't ignore the mounting evidence any longer. A group formed, determined to get to the bottom of the curse that plagued their town. Led by Sarah, a local historian, they delved into the town's dark past in search of answers.

Their research led them to the legend of a powerful witch who had been banished from Ravenswood centuries ago. The witch, known as Morgana, had cursed the town as she was driven out, vowing that misfortune would befall anyone who crossed paths with her familiar—a black cat named Midnight.

As the group delved deeper, they discovered that Midnight had survived the centuries, passing down the curse from one generation to the next. The black cat was not just an ordinary feline but a vessel of dark magic, forever entwined with Morgana's malevolence.

Determined to break the curse, Sarah and her companions embarked on a perilous journey. They sought out ancient grimoires and consulted wise elders, desperate to find a way to lift the curse that had plagued their town for far too long.

Their search led them to a hidden chamber deep within an abandoned cottage on the outskirts of Ravenswood. Within its walls, they discovered a ritual, a complex series of incantations and offerings that could potentially break the curse.

The night of the ritual arrived, the moon casting an eerie glow over the town. Sarah and her companions gathered in a circle, each holding a piece of the black cat's fur—a token of their connection to the curse. They chanted the ancient incantations, their voices trembling with both fear and determination.

As the final syllable left their lips, a gust of wind swept through the chamber, extinguishing the candles. Darkness enveloped them, broken only by the glint of Midnight's eyes. The black cat appeared before them, its body radiating an otherworldly aura.

With a voice filled with anguish, the cat revealed its true nature. It had been bound to

Morgana's curse against its will, longing for liberation from the malevolence that had plagued it for centuries. Midnight pleaded with the group to find a way to break the curse and set it free.

Guided by the cat's desperate plea, Sarah and her companions performed the final steps of the ritual. They burned the pieces of fur, symbolizing the release of the curse's hold. The chamber filled with a blinding light, and the cat's form transformed into that of a woman— Morgana herself.

But this was not the vengeful witch of legend. Morgana's spirit had been trapped within Midnight, cursed to wander through time as a cat. As she regained her human form, tears streamed down her face, a mixture of relief and remorse.

With Morgana's curse finally broken, Ravenswood experienced a change. The air seemed lighter, the gloom lifting. The townsfolk noticed the difference too. The accidents, illnesses, and unexplained deaths stopped. Peace and tranquility returned to Ravenswood.

Morgana, free of the curse at last, disappeared the next day, leaving behind only the black cat, who was now just an ordinary feline. Yet, the townsfolk no longer feared Midnight. Instead, they saw the cat as a symbol of their triumph over the old superstitions that had once controlled them.

Sarah and her group were hailed as heroes. They had faced their fears, delved into their town's dark past, and emerged victorious. The story of their courage was passed down through the generations, forever changing the way Ravenswood thought about black cats.

From that day on, whenever a black cat crossed someone's path in Ravenswood, it was not a sign of impending doom but a reminder of their town's resilience and the power of truth over fear. And as for Midnight, he found a loving home with Sarah, living out the rest of his days as a beloved pet, free from the burdens of the past.

In the end, Ravenswood was a town transformed, a place where old superstitions had been laid to rest and replaced with understanding and acceptance. The tale of the black cat's curse became just a story, a piece of the town's history that served as a reminder of the dangers of letting fear and superstition dictate one's actions.

Now let's break down this superstition of black cats:

The superstition surrounding black cats primarily originates from Western history, particularly during the Middle Ages in Europe. Here are some key points about its backstory, origin, and cultural background:

1. Medieval Europe (Middle Ages):
The superstition around black cats being bad luck primarily stems from the Middle Ages in Europe. During this time, there was a

widespread belief in witchcraft and superstition. Black cats were often associated with witches, believed to be their familiars or even witches themselves transformed into animal form. This association with witchcraft led to the belief that black cats were harbingers of bad luck or evil.

2. The Witch Hunts:

During the witch hunts of the 15th to 18th centuries, the hysteria and paranoia towards witchcraft increased. Black cats, due to their associations with witches, were often killed alongside their supposed human counterparts. This further reinforced the belief in their being bad omens.

3. Sailors and Pirates Superstitions:

Sailors and pirates also held numerous superstitions about black cats. Some believed a black cat aboard a ship would bring good luck, while others thought it would bring disaster. If a black cat walked onto a ship and then walked off again, the ship was doomed to sink on its next voyage.

4. Black Cat and Halloween:

In modern times, especially in the United States, the black cat became a staple of Halloween folklore. This likely stems from the animal's historical association with witchcraft. In Halloween iconography, black cats are often depicted along with witches, ghosts, and other symbols of the supernatural.

Interestingly, not all cultures view black cats as bad luck. For instance:

1. British and Japanese Beliefs:
In British and Japanese folklore, black cats are generally considered good luck. In English lore, giving a bride a black cat as a wedding gift is thought to bring good luck to her marriage. In Japan, black cats are considered good luck and are especially favored by single women, as they are believed to attract potential suitors.

2. Egyptian Reverence:
Ancient Egyptians revered all cats, including black ones, and even had a goddess named Bastet who was depicted as a lioness or as a woman with the head of a lion or a domestic

cat. Killing a cat, even accidentally, was considered a grave sin in this culture.

So while the superstition of black cats being bad luck is prevalent in some cultures, it's not a universal belief and varies greatly around the world.

Friday The 13th

"This date is considered unlucky in Western culture. It's unclear exactly where this superstition comes from, but it could be related to Christian beliefs (there were 13 people at the Last Supper, and the crucifixion happened on a Friday)."

THE HAUNTING OF FRIDAY THE 13th

Charlie stared at the decrepit house that loomed ominously against the backdrop of the full moon. His friends — Julia, Sam, Dustin, and Lydia — huddled close, the apprehension clear on their faces. The chilling wind of the November night added an extra layer of eeriness to the ghostly appearance of the abandoned house.

This was Charlie's idea. An adrenaline junkie, he had suggested they explore the house on this fateful Friday the 13th. A night when the supernatural was said to be at its peak. A night when the veil between the living and the dead was at its thinnest.

As they stepped into the house, the old wooden door creaked shut behind them. A sense of doom filled the air. The house was dark and damp, with cobwebs hanging from the ceiling and the unmistakable scent of mold lingering. They ventured further in, their torches barely illuminating the darkness.

Suddenly, an icy gust swept through the hall. Charlie turned around and found himself alone. His friends had vanished. Confusion turned to panic as he called out their names, but the house swallowed his cries. He felt a sinking feeling in his stomach. Something was horribly wrong.

He stumbled through the house, desperate to find his friends. As he turned a corner, he heard Julia's voice coming from a room. He rushed in, only to see her sobbing uncontrollably. In front of her were images of her late mother, reliving her painful last moments in the hospital. Julia was reliving her worst fear, the loss of her mother.

Charlie tried to comfort her, but she was oblivious to his presence. As he tried to reach out, he was sucked back into the hallway. Feeling helpless, he moved on, only to hear a blood-curdling scream next. He found himself in a room where Sam stood, paralyzed with fear. In front of him was a massive spider, its hairy legs moving menacingly. Sam was arachnophobic.

Again, Charlie was unable to help, pulled away by an invisible force, leaving Sam alone with his fear. The house seemed to be feeding off their emotions, their fears becoming their realities. Dustin was next, trapped in a room with mirrors reflecting his darkest secret — his hidden addiction. Lydia was left alone, tormented by the image of her abusive ex-boyfriend.

Charlie was horrified. This wasn't just an exploration gone wrong. They were trapped in a nightmarish loop. Suddenly, the house seemed to turn its attention towards him. He found himself in a room with pictures of his childhood. The images started to move, showing him the day his younger brother had drowned. It was a day he blamed himself for, a guilt he had carried for years.

Tears streamed down his face as he realized what he was up against. He had to break this loop, but how? As he sobbed, he recalled his grandmother's words about facing one's fears. Was that the key? Could they break free by confronting their fears? The realization hit him like a lightning bolt.

With newfound determination, he ran back to Julia, urging her to face her fear, to accept her mother's death. Slowly, the images started to fade away. He moved on to Sam, Dustin, and Lydia, helping them confront their fears and secrets. As they did, their rooms turned back into normal, dilapidated parts of the house. The malevolent energy seemed to be dissipating.

Finally, he had to face his own fear. He needed to accept that he was not responsible for his brother's death. It was a tragic accident, nothing more. Tears streamed down his face as he let go of the guilt he had held onto for so long. As he did, the room started to fade, the tormenting images disappearing.

Suddenly, the house shook violently. A deafening roar echoed through the halls as the house seemed to convulse in anger. Then, as abruptly as it had started, it stopped. The house was silent, the eerie atmosphere replaced by a sense of calm. The friends found themselves back in the main hall, shaken but safe.

They quickly exited the house, the door creaking open with surprising ease. As they stepped outside, the first rays of the morning sun began to peek over the horizon. It was Saturday the 14th. They had survived the nightmarish loop of Friday the 13th.

Charlie looked back at the house one last time. It was just an abandoned house now, its supernatural power gone. They had faced their worst fears, confronted their darkest secrets, and had come out stronger.

As they walked away, they vowed never to return. The experience had given them a new understanding of fear and the power it held over them. They had faced the darkest parts of their souls, and they were ready to move on, their bonds of friendship stronger than ever. But the memory of that Friday the 13th would forever serve as a chilling reminder of the night they spent in the haunted house.

Now let's break down this superstition of Friday the 13th:

The superstition surrounding the date Friday the 13th comes from various sources and interpretations throughout history. There's no definitive origin, but here are a few possibilities:

1. Biblical References:
One theory suggests the superstition stems from Christian beliefs, particularly related to the Last Supper and the crucifixion of Jesus Christ. At the Last Supper, there were 13 individuals present (Jesus and his 12 apostles), and one of them, Judas, is traditionally regarded as the one who betrayed Jesus.

Additionally, Jesus was crucified on a Friday, which was known as Good Friday. The combination of these two elements - 13 attendees at the Last Supper and the crucifixion on a Friday - may have contributed to the superstition.

2. Knights Templar Arrests:

Another historical event that took place on Friday the 13th was the mass arrest of the Knights Templar. On Friday, October 13, 1307, members of the Knights Templar, a medieval Christian military order, were arrested en masse by King Philip IV of France. This event left a mark on the collective memory and might have contributed to the belief in the unlucky nature of Friday the 13th.

3. Literary Influence:

The superstition was popularized in the 20th century through Thomas W. Lawson's novel "Friday, the Thirteenth" (1907), in which a stockbroker uses the superstition to create a Wall Street panic on a Friday the 13th.

4. Numerological Significance:

The number 13 has been considered unlucky in various cultures, and Friday has been viewed as the week's unluckiest day. The convergence of these two factors on a single date has led to an enduring superstition. In numerology, 12 is considered a number of completeness (12 hours of the clock, 12 months of the year, 12 gods of Olympus, 12 tribes of Israel, etc.), and 13 is seen as transgressing this completeness and therefore is seen as unlucky.

5. Modern Media Influence:
In recent times, the superstition has been amplified by pop culture, most notably through the "Friday the 13th" horror movie franchise, which centers around an unlucky and deadly day at a summer camp.

Like many superstitions, the fear of Friday the 13th (known as paraskevidekatriaphobia) varies widely around the world. In some cultures, other days or numbers are considered more unlucky. For example, in Italy, Friday the 17th is considered unlucky, and in Spain and Greece, Tuesday the 13th is considered a day of bad luck.

Knocking on Wood

"This is done to prevent disappointment or continue a streak of good luck."

TALE OF THE CURSED WOOD

Rebecca had always been a lover of antiquities. She found that being in the presence of items that had witnessed centuries of history gave her a sense of comfort, a connection to the past. One day, while perusing an antique shop in the quiet outskirts of her hometown, she found an intricately carved wooden artifact, an ancient, tribal-looking mask. The shopkeeper told her it was from an old tribe in South America known for its belief in spirits and the afterlife. Rebecca was fascinated and, despite its expensive price tag, she purchased it.

There was a peculiar tradition associated with the mask. "They believed that knocking on it would bring good fortune, miss," the shopkeeper had told her. Rebecca, a bit superstitious herself, took this tradition to heart. Every morning before work, she would give the mask a gentle knock, hoping for a day of good luck.

For the first few days, everything seemed fine. But as days turned into weeks, Rebecca started noticing odd things happening around her house. She would hear strange noises in the middle of the night, like whispers and soft cries. Objects would move from their original places, and she would find doors open that she was sure she had locked.

One night, she woke up to a chilling breeze. She sat upright, her heart pounding. The whispers were louder this time, more desperate, and there was something else, a low, menacing growl that filled her room. Fear crawling up her spine, she turned on the lamp beside her bed. There, in the room corner, was a horrifying shadowy figure, its form shifting and changing, but its eyes, two glowing orbs, were fixed on her.

Rebecca screamed, scrambling out of her bed and darting out of her room. She ran to the living room where the wooden mask was. She didn't know why, but something told her that the mask was connected to this entity. Her mind raced back to the shopkeeper's words, "knocking on it would bring good fortune." Her instincts screamed at her that she had been knocking at something far more malevolent than she had ever dreamed.

Desperate and terrified, she grabbed her phone and dialed the number of a local paranormal investigator, a man named Edgar who was known for his work with spiritual entities. As she waited for Edgar, she sat in the living room, her eyes never leaving the mask.

When Edgar arrived, Rebecca explained the situation, her words tumbling out in a rush. Edgar listened, his eyes hard and serious. He examined the mask and then turned to Rebecca. "This mask," he said, "is not a mere artifact. It's a spirit cage. The tribe who made this used to trap malevolent spirits inside such masks. Every knock you've made has released a part of the spirit."

Rebecca felt her stomach drop. She had been releasing a malevolent entity into her home, all the while thinking she was inviting good fortune. "So, how do we trap it back?" she asked, her voice barely above a whisper.

Edgar explained that they would need to perform a ritual that the tribe used to trap spirits. It wouldn't be easy, and it would require Rebecca's participation since she was the one who had released the spirit. It was a terrifying prospect, but Rebecca knew she had to do it. She could not live in fear, haunted by a spirit she unknowingly released.

That night, under the guidance of Edgar, Rebecca began the ritual. She lit the candles Edgar had brought and arranged them in a circle around the mask. Edgar started chanting in an ancient tongue, the words almost musical in their rhythm. Rebecca joined him, her voice shaky at first but growing steadier as she focused on the task at hand.

The temperature in the room seemed to drop, the air becoming icy cold. The shadowy figure appeared again, its form more terrifying than ever. It seemed to be drawn to the mask but was also resisting, its growls vibrating through the room. Rebecca's heart pounded in her chest as she continued the chant, her gaze fixed on the entity.

Suddenly, the entity lunged at her, but it seemed to hit an invisible barrier around the circle. It recoiled, its growl turning into an ear-splitting screech that made Rebecca's blood run cold. But she didn't stop the chant. She couldn't. She felt a strange energy flowing through her, as if the words she was saying were giving her strength.

After what felt like an eternity, the entity started to shrink, its form becoming less substantial. It was being drawn into the mask, piece by piece, just as it had been released. The room filled with a blinding light, and then, as suddenly as it had started, everything stopped. The entity was gone, the mask was still, and the room was back to normal.

Rebecca slumped to the floor, exhaustion washing over her. Edgar helped her up, his face pale but relieved. "You did it," he said. "You trapped the spirit back into the mask."

In the days that followed, Rebecca's home returned to normal, the strange occurrences ceased, and she could sleep without fear. She kept the mask, a reminder of the danger she had unknowingly invited and the strength she had found within herself to overcome it. But she never knocked on it again. The traditional good luck charm had turned into a symbol of her terrifying encounter, a relic of the past that held a malevolent spirit captive.

Rebecca learned a valuable lesson that day, one that she carried with her throughout her life: not everything that seems to bring good fortune is as benign as it seems. In the end, it was not luck but her courage that saved her from the horrifying entity she had released. And that courage was something no knock on an ancient artifact could ever give her.

Now let's break down this superstition of knocking on wood:

The superstition of "knocking on wood" or "touching wood" is a widely practiced tradition that aims to prevent disappointment or maintain good luck. The origins of this superstition can be traced back to various cultural beliefs and folklore. Here's an exploration of its backstory, origin, and cultural background:

1. Tree Spirits and Good Luck:
One of the most commonly suggested origins of "knocking on wood" is linked to ancient pagan beliefs. Many cultures held the belief that spirits or deities resided within trees, which were considered sacred. These spirits were believed to bring good fortune and protection. By touching or knocking on wood, people sought to invoke the favor and protection of these benevolent spirits.

2. Warding off Evil Spirits:

Another interpretation of the tradition involves the belief in evil spirits or mischievous supernatural beings. It was believed that these entities often listened to conversations, waiting for an opportunity to bring bad luck or ill fortune. Knocking on or touching wood was thought to create a noise that would distract or ward off these malevolent spirits, ensuring the continuation of good luck or preventing the jinxing of a positive situation.

3. Christian Influence:
In Christian folklore, wood carried religious significance. The cross of Jesus Christ, upon which he was crucified, was made of wood. Touching or knocking on wood became associated with seeking divine protection and invoking the power of the cross to ward off evil or protect against misfortune.

4. Ancient Rituals and Beliefs:
The practice of touching or knocking on wood can also be seen as a remnant of ancient rituals and beliefs. It is believed that some cultures, such as the ancient Celts, would touch or tap sacred trees to express gratitude or make

wishes. This act was seen as a way to connect with the spiritual realm and seek blessings.

Over time, the tradition of "knocking on wood" has become deeply ingrained in Western culture and is often done reflexively, even by individuals who may not hold strong beliefs in its supernatural origins. The act has become a popular way to express a desire to maintain good luck or to prevent the jinxing of a positive outcome.

It's worth noting that variations of this superstition exist in different cultures around the world. For example, in some cultures, people may "knock on wood" by spitting, blowing, or making a hand gesture instead of physically touching wood.

Opening an Umbrella Indoors

"This is thought to bring bad luck, possibly because it could poke someone in the eye or break something in the house."

THE HIDDEN UMBRELLA

Carson and his family had recently moved into a charming old house nestled in a quiet neighborhood. Excitement filled the air as they unpacked boxes and began settling into their new home. While exploring the attic, Carson stumbled upon a dusty chest tucked away in a corner. Intrigued, he opened it and found an old, tattered umbrella.

Unbeknownst to Carson and his family, this seemingly harmless umbrella held a dark secret. It had been hidden away for a reason, for opening it indoors would awaken a curse that summoned a relentless poltergeist.

Oblivious to the impending danger, Carson decided to keep the umbrella as a quirky decoration in his room.

That night, as the clock struck midnight, strange occurrences began to unfold. Whispers echoed through the hallways, and objects started moving on their own. The air grew heavy with an eerie chill, and an unsettling presence permeated every corner of the house. Carson's family dismissed these incidents as mere coincidences, attributing them to the house's age and unfamiliarity.

However, as days turned into weeks, the poltergeist's actions grew more sinister. Furniture would be violently thrown across rooms, shattering against the walls. Unseen hands would tug at the family members' clothes, leaving them with scratches and bruises. Terrifying laughter echoed through the night, making it impossible for anyone to find solace in sleep.

Carson, plagued by fear, began to connect the haunting to the umbrella he had discovered. The realization struck him like a bolt of lightning, piercing through the darkness of his mind. He knew that the curse had been awakened by his unsuspecting act of opening the umbrella indoors.

Determined to put an end to the torment, Carson sought the help of a renowned paranormal investigator named Dr. Lawrence. With a mix of skepticism and curiosity, Dr. Lawrence agreed to assist Carson and his family in breaking the curse.

Together, they embarked on a perilous journey to unravel the secrets behind the cursed umbrella. The investigator delved into ancient texts and dusty archives, unearthing the tragic history of the umbrella's previous owners. It had been used as a tool of dark magic, and the curse had plagued generations before it was sealed away.

Dr. Lawrence devised a risky plan to banish the poltergeist and break the curse. It involved a complex ritual that required the family's unwavering courage and unity. They had to confront the malevolent spirit head-on, facing their deepest fears and standing strong in the face of its relentless attacks.

The night of the ritual arrived, and Carson's family gathered in the heart of their haunted home. Dr. Lawrence guided them through the intricate steps, invoking ancient incantations and symbols. As they chanted, the poltergeist manifested before them, a swirling vortex of rage and anguish.

In a battle of wills and determination, Carson's family stood firm, refusing to succumb to the spirit's intimidation. Their love for one another and their unwavering resolve weakened the curse's grip. The power of unity and bravery proved to be the family's greatest weapon against the forces of darkness.

With a final surge of energy, they succeeded in banishing the poltergeist back to the shadows from whence it came. The house fell silent, the air cleared, and the weight of the curse lifted. Carson and his family were finally free from the haunting that had plagued them.

As time passed, the house became a place of warmth and tranquility once again. Carson's family found solace in the fact that they had overcome the curse, emerging stronger and closer than ever before. They decided to keep the umbrella as a reminder of their triumph over darkness, a symbol of their resilience and unity.

Carson learned a valuable lesson from this harrowing experience. He understood the importance of being mindful of the objects we bring into our lives and the significance of ancient artifacts. He vowed to treat every item with caution and respect, aware that even the most innocuous-looking objects could hold hidden secrets and unleash unforeseen consequences.

The memory of the haunting lingered in their minds, a reminder of the fragility of the barrier between the living and the supernatural. Carson's family embraced a newfound appreciation for their home, grateful for the peace they had regained and the bond that had grown stronger through adversity.

In the years that followed, Carson shared his story with others, cautioning them about the dangers of opening mysterious objects and the importance of understanding the history behind them. His tale served as a chilling reminder to respect the boundaries of the unknown, to tread carefully in the realm of the supernatural.

As for the cursed umbrella, it remained a silent sentinel, a testament to the power of human resilience and the triumph of light over darkness. Carson's family kept it locked away, a reminder of their shared journey and the strength they had discovered within themselves.

And so, Carson's family moved forward, forever changed by the haunting and yet forever united. They carried the lessons learned from their encounter with the poltergeist, cherishing the newfound appreciation for the safety and love within the walls of their home. They would forever remember the haunting as a testament to the power of love, courage, and the indomitable human spirit.

Now let's break down this superstition of opening an umbrella indoors:

The superstition of opening an umbrella indoors and it being perceived as bad luck is steeped in various cultural backstories and origins. Here are a few interpretations:

1. Ancient Egyptian Symbolism:
Umbrellas or parasols were used in Ancient Egypt not just to provide shade but also as a symbol of protection and status, often associated with the gods and goddesses. Opening these symbolic items indoors, away from the sun, was seen as an insult to the sun god Ra, thus attracting bad luck.

2. Victorian England:
During the Victorian era, metal-spoked waterproof umbrellas became popular. However, the spring mechanism was quite powerful. Opening one indoors could have caused a serious injury to people or damage to fragile objects in the house. Therefore, it became associated with bad luck and

misfortune, possibly as a deterrent to prevent such accidents.

3. Spiritual Protection:

There are also theories that umbrellas were considered as a shield against the sun, but also as a shield against evil spirits in some cultures. Opening an umbrella indoors was seen as a sign of disrespect to protective spirits dwelling in the house, inviting them to leave and thus removing a layer of protection.

It's important to note that with many superstitions, the origins are often difficult to pinpoint with certainty, and the true beginnings could be a blend of many different beliefs and practices. Over time, these superstitions are passed down through generations and can become embedded in cultural norms and traditions.

Spilling Salt

"Spilling salt is considered bad luck in many cultures. In the past, salt was a valuable commodity, so wasting it was seen as wasteful and unlucky. Some people toss a pinch over their left shoulder to ward off any bad luck."

THE SALTED SHADOW

Keely had always been a bit skeptical about old wives' tales, myths, and superstitions until that fateful night when she accidentally knocked over a salt shaker at the dinner table. Her grandmother, a woman of Irish descent, was a firm believer in such traditions and would often regale Keely with tales of mischievous leprechauns, lurking banshees, and ominous omens.

"One should never spill salt, Keely," she'd warn with a serious look in her eyes. "And if you do, always throw some over your left shoulder. It's to blind the devil that sits there."

Keely would laugh at these stories, finding them nothing more than amusing folklore. However, that night after the spilt salt, she didn't laugh. She didn't throw a pinch over her left shoulder either. Instead, she cleaned up the salt, shaking her head at the absurdity of the superstition.

The next morning, Keely woke up to find her apartment in disarray. Her furniture was overturned, her clothes strewn across the floor, and her dishes shattered in the sink. She was sure she had locked her doors and windows the previous night, yet there was no sign of a break-in.

Over the next few days, things began to escalate. There were accidents, near-misses with cars, random objects falling from shelves just as she passed. Each event was more dangerous than the last, and Keely found herself looking over her shoulder more often than not. She felt a presence, a malicious entity that seemed to be growing stronger with each passing day.

One night, after narrowly avoiding a falling chandelier, Keely decided to visit her grandmother. The old woman listened intently as Keely recounted the series of bizarre accidents. With a grim look on her face, she took Keely's hand.

"The spirit of chaos has found you, child," she said, her voice trembling. "It feeds off disorder, revels in turmoil. When you spilt that salt and didn't heed the old ways, you invited it in."

"But how do I get rid of it, Gran?" Keely asked, her heart pounding in her chest.

Her grandmother sighed heavily, "Salt is a powerful element, my dear. It's a protector, a purifier. We must perform a cleansing ritual."

Following her grandmother's instructions, Keely spent the next day preparing for the ritual. She lined her doorways with salt, lit white candles, and recited an ancient prayer. That night, as she sat in the center of her salt circle, she felt a cold breeze sweep through her apartment. She could sense the entity, its anger at her attempt to banish it.

Suddenly, a powerful gust of wind extinguished the candles, plunging the room into darkness. The deafening silence was broken only by the faint sound of salt crunching under invisible footsteps. Keely could feel her heart pounding in her ears as the temperature dropped further, her breath visible in the icy air.

Then, it appeared. A shadowy figure, its form barely distinguishable in the darkness. It moved around the salt circle, a low growl emanating from it. Keely steeled herself, repeating the prayer her grandmother had taught her.

"Be gone, spirit of chaos! I deny you my fear, I deny you my home!" she shouted into the darkness.

The entity roared with a sound that made the walls of her apartment shudder. In response, Keely shouted the prayer louder, her voice echoing through the room. The shadowy figure seemed to recoil, its form wavering as if in pain.

"I deny you my fear, I deny you my home!" Keely repeated, her voice shaking but determined.

Suddenly, a brilliant light burst forth from the salt circle, illuminating the room. The entity shrieked, its form disintegrating into a whirling mass of shadows before disappearing entirely. The light receded, leaving only the flickering candles and the faint smell of salt in the air.

Keely sat in stunned silence, her heart pounding. The oppressive dread that had filled her apartment was gone, replaced by a peaceful calm. She felt a wave of relief wash over her, bringing tears to her eyes. The spirit of chaos was banished, the superstition was real.

Over the next few days, life returned to normal for Keely. The accidents ceased, the presence was gone, and her apartment felt like a home again. She visited her grandmother, recounting her harrowing experience.

"I'm proud of you, Keely," her grandmother said, a warm smile on her face. "You stood up to your fear and sent that spirit packing. I hope you've learned the importance of our old ways."

Keely nodded, "I have, Gran. No more spilled salt for me. And if I do, I'll remember to throw some over my left shoulder."

From that day forward, Keely respected the superstitions she once laughed at. She understood their power, their significance. And whenever she saw a salt shaker, she couldn't help but remember the shadowy figure, the spirit of chaos that had once haunted her. She knew she'd never forget the lesson she'd learned: some traditions, no matter how old or seemingly absurd, hold more truth than meets the eye.

Now let's break down this superstition of spilling salt:

The superstition surrounding spilling salt and its association with bad luck can be traced back to several cultural beliefs and historical contexts. Here are a few interpretations:

1. Ancient Rome:

In ancient Rome, salt was a highly prized and valuable commodity. It was believed that spilling salt was an omen of misfortune because of its scarcity and significance. It was also associated with Judas Iscariot, the betrayer of Jesus in Christian tradition, as Leonardo da Vinci's painting "The Last Supper" depicts Judas knocking over a salt shaker.

2. Medieval Times:

During the medieval period, salt was considered a powerful and protective substance. It was believed to have purifying qualities and was often used in religious rituals. Spilling salt was seen as a violation of its sacred nature and was thought to attract evil spirits or demons. The act of throwing a pinch of salt over the left shoulder was believed to blind the demons or evil spirits, protecting the person from their influence.

3. Naval Superstitions:

 Another interpretation of the salt-spilling superstition comes from naval traditions. Salt was a valuable commodity on ships, and spilling it was considered an ill omen. It was believed that if salt was spilled, it could lead to conflicts or even shipwrecks. To counteract the bad luck, sailors would throw a pinch of salt over their left shoulder, symbolically blinding the devil and preventing disaster.

It's worth noting that superstitions can vary across cultures and regions, and different explanations may exist for the same belief. As with many superstitions, the specific origins can be challenging to trace definitively, but these cultural and historical contexts provide some insight into the belief surrounding spilling salt.

Crossing Fingers

Curse of the Clenched Fingers

Colby had always been a hopeful person, a dreamer with an unwavering belief in the power of wishes. He would often find himself crossing his fingers, silently whispering his desires into the universe, hoping that they would come true. Little did he know that one day, his wishful thinking would unleash a nightmare beyond his imagination.

It started innocently enough. Colby was having a particularly bad day at work when he decided to escape into the solace of his thoughts. He closed his eyes, crossed his fingers, and wished for everything to get better. To his astonishment, the very next day, his boss announced a surprise promotion for him. It was as if his wish had been granted.

Overjoyed by this newfound power, Colby began making wishes more frequently. He wished for wealth, and a lottery ticket he bought on a whim won him a substantial sum of money. He wished for love, and he soon found himself in a passionate and fulfilling relationship. It seemed that his wishes were coming true, and life couldn't have been better.

But as the days went on, Colby noticed that his wishes were taking a sinister turn. The nightmares began subtly, with a slight twist to his desires. He wished for success in his career, but with every promotion, he found himself burdened with mounting responsibilities and unbearable stress. He wished for love, but his relationship turned toxic, filled with manipulation and deceit.

Terrified and confused, Colby tried to rationalize these nightmarish outcomes. Perhaps it was mere coincidence or a result of his own subconscious fears. Still, deep down, he couldn't shake the feeling that there was something more insidious at play.

Undeterred by the nightmares, Colby continued to make wishes, hoping to reverse the curse that had befallen him. He wished for happiness, but his days were filled with unrelenting sorrow and despair. He wished for peace of mind, but his thoughts became a chaotic whirlwind of anxiety and paranoia. Each wish he made only intensified the horror that awaited him.

With his sanity hanging by a thread, Colby decided to seek help. He consulted mystics, spiritual healers, and even psychologists, but none could provide an explanation or a solution to his torment. It seemed that he was trapped in a nightmarish cycle, forever bound by his own desires.

As Colby's life spiraled further into darkness, he realized that he had to confront the source of his suffering. Gathering every ounce of courage he had left, he closed his eyes, crossed his fingers one last time, and wished for the nightmare to end. This time, instead of a wish, he whispered a plea into the void.

In that moment, the room filled with an eerie silence. The nightmares ceased, the twisted desires faded away, and Colby felt a weight lift off his shoulders. He had broken free from the curse that had consumed his life.

From that day forward, Colby abandoned his belief in wishes and the power they held. He focused on rebuilding his life, learning to appreciate the simple joys and embracing the unpredictable nature of reality. The nightmares served as a haunting reminder of the dangers of unchecked desires and the importance of finding contentment in the present.

And as for crossing fingers, Colby vowed to keep his hands open, ready to embrace life's uncertainties, knowing that true happiness lay not in wishes, knowing that true happiness lay not in wishes, but in acceptance and gratitude for what he already had.

Years passed, and Colby carried the scars of his ordeal as a reminder of the dangers that lurk in the depths of one's desires. He became an advocate for mindfulness and self-reflection, sharing his story with others who found themselves trapped in the cycle of wishful thinking.

But deep down, he couldn't help but wonder about the origin of the curse. Was it a mere coincidence, or was there a force beyond his understanding at play? He delved into ancient texts and sought out the wisdom of sages and scholars, hoping to uncover the truth.

Eventually, his quest led him to a reclusive mystic who claimed to possess knowledge of the dark arts. With trepidation, Colby approached the mystic, sharing his story and seeking answers.

The mystic listened intently, his eyes filled with a mix of sorrow and understanding. "You have become entangled in the realm of the trickster spirits," he said in a hushed voice. "When we wish without caution, we invite chaos into our lives. The desires we hold dear can be twisted and perverted, leading us down a path of nightmares."

Colby's heart sank as he realized the truth. The power of wishes was real, but it came with a price. The mystic offered a final piece of advice, "To break the curse, you must learn to tame your desires and find balance within yourself. Only then will the spirits release their grip on your life."

With newfound determination, Colby embarked on a journey of self-discovery. He engaged in meditation, practiced gratitude, and embraced the beauty of the present moment. Slowly but surely, the nightmares faded away, and a sense of peace enveloped his existence.

As the years went by, Colby became a beacon of hope for those who had fallen victim to their own wishes. He shared his story, cautioning others about the dangers of unchecked desires and the importance of finding fulfillment within. His experiences served as a reminder that true happiness is not found in the fulfillment of every wish, but in the cultivation of inner peace and contentment.

And so, Colby walked his path, carrying the scars of his journey as a testament to the power of self-awareness. The nightmares had transformed him, shaping him into a wiser, more compassionate soul. And as he watched the sunset, he couldn't help but feel grateful for the lessons he had learned, for they had forged him into the person he was meant to be.

Now let's break down this superstition of crossing fingers:

The act of crossing fingers as a gesture to wish for good luck has a long history and can be traced back to various cultural and historical origins. While the exact origin of this superstition is not definitively known, here are a couple of interpretations:

1. Early Christianity:
One theory suggests that crossing fingers originated from early Christianity. In Christian tradition, the sign of the cross is a powerful symbol representing protection and invoking

divine intervention. It is possible that people, when unable to physically make the sign of the cross, started crossing their fingers as a symbolic gesture to call upon the power and blessings associated with the Christian cross.

2. Pre-Christian Beliefs:
Another theory suggests that crossing fingers predates Christianity and has roots in pre-Christian pagan beliefs. Some ancient cultures believed that crossing two fingers formed a protective barrier against evil spirits or bad luck. By crossing their fingers, individuals may have sought to ward off misfortune or to invoke the assistance of benevolent deities or supernatural forces.

It's important to note that the origins of this superstition might be more complex and varied, and it could have evolved over time through a combination of cultural influences and personal interpretations. Additionally, crossing fingers is also commonly done as a gesture of hope or to express a desire for luck, irrespective of any specific religious or cultural belief.

Overall, the exact origins of crossing fingers remain somewhat uncertain, but it has become a widely recognized and practiced superstition across various cultures as a way to express positive wishes or invoke good luck.

Rabbit's Foot

"Carrying a rabbit's foot is often considered a good luck charm. "

The Rabbit's Foot

Oryan's life wasn't always so exciting. He was an average teen, attending school, working a part-time job at the local grocery store, and mostly keeping to himself. However, everything changed the day he found the rabbit's foot charm.

Oryan discovered the charm on a peculiar day when he had decided to take a different route home through the woods. It was an odd little thing, covered in soft white fur with a small gold cap and a chain attached. He picked it up, intrigued, and decided to keep it. He had heard the old tales about rabbit's foot charms bringing luck, but he had never been one for superstitions.

The very next day, Oryan experienced his first stroke of luck. He found a fifty-dollar bill on the street, got a surprise raise at work, and managed to ace a test he was sure he would fail. It was a wonderful day, the best he had ever had, and he couldn't help but attribute his good fortune to the rabbit's foot charm.

Days turned into weeks, and Oryan's luck only improved. He was winning contests, getting perfect scores, even the girl he had been secretly admiring asked him out. Life was perfect. But every night when he went to sleep, he was plagued by the same eerie dream. In his dream, he was standing in a dark forest, and a shadowy figure would approach him, whispering in a voice that sounded like rustling leaves, "Payment is due, Oryan."

Oryan initially dismissed the dreams, attributing them to stress and his own overactive imagination. Still, the dreams persisted, growing more intense and unsettling each time. The figure became more defined, clearly not human, its eyes two burning embers in the darkness. It would extend a gnarled hand towards Oryan, insisting on its payment.

Then came the day when Oryan's luck started to sour. It began with small misfortunes like losing his keys or spilling his coffee, but it soon escalated. He was failing tests, his girlfriend broke up with him, he lost his job, and soon, his life seemed to be spiraling out of control.

He started to connect the dots and realized that his misfortunes began the same day his dreams had become nightmares. The rabbit's foot, once a symbol of fortune, now felt like a cold, hard stone in his pocket. He tried to get rid of it, but no matter where he left it, it would always find its way back to him.

One night, in his dream, the figure finally revealed its true form. It was a grotesque creature, its body a twisted parody of a rabbit's, standing on its hind legs. Its eyes were like burning coals, and its voice was like a rasping wind through a graveyard. "Payment is due, Oryan," it said, its voice echoing through the darkness. "Your luck was not for free, and the price must be paid."

Oryan woke up in a cold sweat, the rabbit's foot charm burning hot in his hand. He knew what he had to do. He had to return the charm to the place where he found it.

He ventured into the woods, the night air biting at his skin. His heart pounded in his chest as he made his way to the spot. He could feel the creature watching him, its presence looming over him like a thundercloud. He placed the rabbit's foot on the ground and stepped back, his breath hitching in the cold air. Suddenly, the forest around him fell silent. The wind stopped, and the trees seemed to hold their breath. Then, a rustling sound filled his ears, growing louder until it was all he could hear.

From the shadows, the creature revealed itself. Its eyes glowed like smoldering coals in the darkness, and its body, a grotesque mockery of a rabbit's, towered over Oryan. He could feel its rage, its powerful desire for the payment it was owed.

"Here," Oryan stammered, gesturing towards the rabbit's foot. "Take it back. I don't want your luck."

The creature extended a gnarled, claw-like hand and picked up the charm. Its gaze never left Oryan's, studying him, measuring him. Then, it spoke, its voice a chilling echo in the silent forest. "The debt is paid."

And just like that, the creature was gone. The forest came back to life, the wind rustling the leaves and the night sounds filling the air once again. Oryan was alone, the weight of the rabbit's foot no longer in his pocket.

Oryan returned home, feeling as though he had awoken from a long, terrifying dream. His life returned to normal, or at least as normal as it could be after such an experience. He started to rebuild, to pick up the pieces that the charm had shattered.

He never forgot the creature, though. He remembered its words, the price he had paid for his fleeting fortune. The rabbit's foot charm had brought him luck, but it had come at a sinister price. A price Oryan was lucky to escape from.

From then on, Oryan was careful what he wished for, and he lived his life with a newfound appreciation for ordinary days and simpler fortunes. He knew that a charm, no matter how lucky, was no substitute for a life honestly lived. And every time he came across a rabbit's foot, he felt a shiver of dread, a reminder of the cost of fortune—and the dark force that demanded payment.

Now let's break down this superstition of the rabbit's foot:

The superstition surrounding the rabbit's foot as a good luck charm has various mythical backstories, origins, and cultural backgrounds. While the exact origins are unclear and subject to speculation, the rabbit's foot as a talisman has been associated with different cultures and belief systems throughout history.

1.Celtic Beliefs:
One possible origin of this superstition can be traced back to ancient Celtic tribes. The Celts

revered animals and believed that they possessed inherent magical qualities. The rabbit, with its ability to reproduce rapidly, was considered a symbol of fertility and abundance. It was believed that carrying a rabbit's foot would bring good luck and increase one's chances of having a prosperous and fertile life.

2.African-American Culture:

In African-American folklore, the superstition of the rabbit's foot is often associated with Hoodoo or conjure traditions. Hoodoo is a folk magic practice that originated among African slaves in the Southern United States. According to this belief system, the left hind foot of a rabbit is particularly potent as a good luck charm. It was believed that the rabbit's foot could ward off evil spirits, bring good fortune, and provide protection.

3.European Beliefs:

Within European folklore, rabbits have been associated with various mythological figures and beliefs. In some European cultures, it was believed that witches could shape-shift into rabbits. Consequently, the foot of a rabbit was seen as a powerful object that could counteract the negative influence of witches and bring good luck. Additionally, the association of rabbits with Easter and the Easter Bunny in Christian traditions may have contributed to the rabbit's foot becoming a symbol of luck and fertility.

Over time, the superstition surrounding the rabbit's foot as a good luck charm has become widespread and has transcended cultural boundaries. It is often seen as a general symbol of good fortune, prosperity, and protection against misfortune. However, it's important to note that superstitions and their origins can vary across different cultures and regions, and the specific beliefs associated with the rabbit's foot may differ accordingly.

It's essential to approach superstitions with an understanding of their cultural context and historical significance. While many people still consider the rabbit's foot a lucky charm, it's ultimately a matter of personal belief and interpretation.

Four-leaf Clover

"Finding a four-leaf clover is considered good luck. The rarity of finding one makes them special. Each leaf is said to symbolize faith, hope, love, and luck. "

The Hidden Field of Clovers

Annette, Simieon, April, and Damien were the best of friends. They were adventurous, always seeking out new experiences and hidden treasures. One sunny afternoon, while exploring a dense forest near their town, they stumbled upon a hidden field unlike anything they had ever seen before.

The field was filled with vibrant green patches, each adorned with a shimmering four-leaf clover. Excitement surged through the group as they realized the significance of their discovery. Four-leaf clovers were symbols of good luck, and finding such a vast collection was an extraordinary stroke of fortune.

Annette was the first to reach down and pluck a clover, a wide smile spreading across her face. Simieon, April, and Damien followed suit, each carefully selecting their own lucky charm. They celebrated their newfound fortune, unaware of the ancient magic they had awakened.

Little did they know, the field of four-leaf clovers was the domain of a vengeful leprechaun named Seamus. The clovers were not mere plants, but rather the leprechaun's precious treasures, stolen from him long ago. His power had remained dormant until the moment the friends had disturbed his sacred land.

As the days passed, the group started experiencing an abundance of good luck. Annette aced all her exams, Simieon won a scholarship, April's art was recognized and featured in a gallery, and Damien's favorite sports team won every match. They reveled in their newfound success, attributing it all to the extraordinary power of the four-leaf clovers.

But as their luck continued to flourish, a series of strange events began to unfold. Annette noticed fleeting shadows in her room at night, whispering voices that seemed to call her name. Simieon's dreams turned into nightmares, with vivid images of a mischievous figure lurking in the shadows. April's artwork took a dark turn, depicting twisted creatures and haunting landscapes. Damien's winning streak came at a price, as injuries plagued his teammates in increasingly bizarre accidents.

Annette, Simieon, April, and Damien grew anxious, realizing that their good luck had come at a cost. They gathered, sharing their haunting experiences and piecing together the connection to the field of four-leaf clovers. Deep down, they knew they had trespassed upon something ancient and powerful.

Determined to make amends, the friends returned to the field, their hearts pounding with trepidation. The once vibrant green patches now seemed withered and lifeless, a stark contrast to their initial discovery. It was there that they encountered Seamus, the leprechaun, his eyes blazing with fury.

"You dare steal my treasures?" Seamus's voice echoed through the air, filled with bitterness and rage. "You shall pay the price for your greed!"

Annette, Simieon, April, and Damien pleaded for forgiveness, explaining their ignorance and promising to return the stolen clovers. But Seamus was unforgiving, his desire for revenge overpowering any sense of mercy. He summoned a tempest of swirling winds and enchanted clovers, trapping the friends within a vortex of chaos.

In a desperate attempt to break free, the friends called upon their bravery and resourcefulness. Annette remembered an old story about leprechauns being appeased by riddles, while Simieon recalled a tale of breaking curses through selfless acts. April used her artistic imagination to conjure a shield of light, and

Damien tapped into his athletic prowess to dodge the swirling clovers.

Together, they devised a plan. Annette stepped forward, her voice steady and determined. "Seamus," she called out, "we didn't realize the significance of what we had taken. We apologize and offer to return your treasures. Please, release us from this torment."

Seamus paused, his anger momentarily subsiding. He peered at the group, considering their words. After a tense moment, he nodded, recognizing the sincerity in their plea. The swirling vortex gradually dissipated, and the field of clovers regained its vibrancy.

In a solemn procession, Annette, Simieon, April, and Damien carefully placed the four-leaf clovers back into the ground, one by one. As the last clover touched the earth, a warm, golden light enveloped the field, and Seamus's features softened.

"You have shown remorse and rectified your mistake," Seamus spoke, his voice filled with a mixture of relief and gratitude. "May this be a lesson learned, and may your lives be filled with true fortune, earned through integrity and kindness."

With those words, Seamus vanished, leaving the friends in the now peaceful field. They took a moment to reflect on the ordeal they had faced, realizing the importance of respecting ancient magic and the consequences of their actions.

From that day forward, Annette, Simieon, April, and Damien carried with them the lessons learned from their encounter with Seamus. They appreciated the true value of good fortune, earned through hard work, kindness, and respect for the powers that governed the world.

As time passed, their lives flourished, not through stolen luck, but through their own efforts and the bonds they shared. And whenever they stumbled upon a four-leaf clover, they would smile, acknowledging the delicate balance between fortune and responsibility, forever mindful of the vengeful leprechaun they had encountered in the hidden field of four-leaf clovers.

Now let's break down this superstition of the four-leaf clover:

The belief that finding a four-leaf clover brings good luck is a superstition that has been passed down through generations and is prevalent in many cultures. Here's some information about the mythical backstory and cultural significance surrounding the four-leaf clover:

1. Celtic and Druidic Beliefs:
The four-leaf clover has connections to ancient Celtic and Druidic beliefs. These cultures considered the clover a sacred plant with mystical properties. It was believed that the rare four-leaf clover possessed magical qualities and could ward off evil spirits or bring good fortune to the finder.

2. Christian Symbolism:

With the spread of Christianity, the four-leaf clover became associated with religious symbolism. Each leaf of the clover was believed to represent a different virtue. The three common leaves stood for faith, hope, and love, while the rare fourth leaf represented luck or God's grace.

3. Irish Folklore:

The association between Ireland and four-leaf clovers is particularly strong. According to Irish folklore, finding a four-leaf clover is said to bring extraordinary luck. It was believed that the clovers were associated with leprechauns, mischievous mythical creatures who would use their magic to hide a pot of gold at the end of a rainbow. Finding a four-leaf clover was believed to increase the likelihood of stumbling upon this hidden treasure.

The rarity of four-leaf clovers, with only about one in every 10,000 clovers having the extra leaf, contributes to their perceived specialness and luck-bringing properties.

It's important to note that the belief in the good luck associated with four-leaf clovers is primarily rooted in folklore and cultural traditions, rather than any concrete evidence. Nevertheless, the four-leaf clover has become a widely recognized symbol of luck and is often sought after by individuals hoping to experience good fortune.

Seeing a Shooting Star

"It's often said that making a wish on a shooting star will make it come true because the star is seen as a falling deity that can fulfill wishes. "

When you wish upon a star

Celine had always been a dreamer, her eyes shining brightly each time she looked up at the night sky. But she never thought that she would live to see the day when one of her wishes would come true. She had wished upon a shooting star, a seemingly harmless and innocent act, yet one that would soon change her life in ways she could never have imagined.

One chilly November night, while sitting on the porch of her secluded country house, she saw a shooting star blaze across the sky. The sky was a velvet canvas, peppered with twinkling stars, and the moon was just a sliver, its silver glow casting long, eerie shadows. The shooting star was so bright, so close, it seemed as though she could reach out and touch it. Celine closed her eyes and made a wish, the same wish she had been making since she was a little girl.

"I wish to not be alone anymore," she whispered into the chilly night.

The next day, she met a man named Vincent. He was charming, handsome, and seemed to understand Celine in a way no one else ever had. They quickly fell in love, and Celine's lonely days became a thing of the past. But soon, she began to notice strange occurrences. Vincent would disappear for hours, leaving Celine alone and worried.

He would return with no explanation, his clothes often dirt-stained and his demeanor distant and cold. One night, she woke up to find him standing over her, his eyes glowing in the dark. Fear gripped her heart, but she convinced herself it was just a trick of the light.

A month later, she spotted another shooting star. Still shaken from her experiences, she hesitated but then made a wish, hoping it would fix everything.

"I wish Vincent would tell me the truth."

The very next day, Vincent confessed. He had been visiting his late wife's grave, unable to let her go. The realization hit Celine like a punch to the gut. But the confession didn't stop there. Vincent revealed he was the one who killed his wife, driven by jealousy and rage. He showed remorse, but the confession chilled Celine to her core. She was living with a murderer.

In a state of panic, Celine ran. She ran until she was far away, hidden in a small motel at the edge of town. She stayed there, alone and terrified. That night, another shooting star streaked across the sky. She knew she shouldn't, but she was desperate.

"I wish Vincent was gone," she whispered.

The next morning, the news of Vincent's sudden death spread through the town. He had been killed in a car accident, a freak event that left no survivors. Celine was relieved but also horrified. Her wishes, they were coming true, but they brought along a terrifying consequence.

Months passed, and Celine lived in terror, avoiding the night sky, the stars, and the curse they held. She moved to the city, surrounded herself with people, and tried to forget. But the fear was always there, lurking in the shadows. Yet, life had a cruel way of twisting her fate.

One night, during a citywide blackout, she found herself alone on her apartment balcony. The city was pitch black, and the stars were unusually bright. Before she could retreat, she saw it—a shooting star, bright and quick, streaking across the sky. Despite herself, a wish slipped from her lips, born from exhaustion and a desperate longing for normalcy.

"I wish to be free of this curse," Celine whispered, her voice trembling.

The next morning, Celine woke up to a world that was eerily silent. She stepped outside her apartment, and the city was deserted. Cars sat abandoned in the streets, their doors left ajar. Shops were empty, their lights flickering eerily. The entire city was devoid of life. Her wish had come true. She was free from the curse of the shooting stars, but at a horrifying cost. She was now completely alone in the world.

As the days turned into weeks, and then into months, Celine's loneliness became unbearable. She wandered the empty streets, her footsteps echoing off the silent buildings. She shouted into the void, her voice bouncing back to her in a cacophony of echoes. But there was no one to hear her, no one to see her.

One night, as she sat on the rooftop of her apartment building, looking up at the starry sky, she saw a shooting star. It was the first one since that fateful night. She knew she shouldn't make a wish, but she was desperate, driven to the brink by her solitude.

"I wish for everything to go back to the way it was," Celine whispered, her voice barely audible.

But the next morning, the world was still empty. She was still alone. The shooting stars had stopped granting her wishes. They had given her what she first asked for, and now they had taken it all away.

Celine was left alone, a single soul in a world devoid of life, a terrifying consequence of a wish made upon a shooting star. She was forced to live in her self-created purgatory, questioning the price she had paid for her desires. It was a chilling reminder of the old saying, "Be careful what you wish for, you just might get it."

And as the years passed, Celine would look up at the night sky, at the twinkling stars, and the occasional shooting star, a silent plea in her heart. But she never made a wish again, for she knew the terrifying consequences all too well.

Now let's break down this superstition of seeing a shooting star:

The belief in making wishes upon seeing a shooting star is a popular superstition that has fascinated people across various cultures throughout history. Here's some information about the mythical backstory and cultural significance surrounding seeing a shooting star:

1. Ancient Greek and Roman Mythology: In ancient Greek and Roman mythology, shooting stars were often associated with the gods and goddesses. They were seen as celestial beings or deities moving across the sky. It was believed that when a shooting star streaked across the heavens, it represented a god or goddess descending from the heavens to Earth. People would make wishes in the belief that these divine beings had the power to grant them.

2. Folklore and Folk Beliefs:

Across different cultures, shooting stars have been linked to various folklore and folk beliefs. In some cultures, shooting stars were considered to be the souls of the departed or spirits passing by. Making a wish on a shooting star was believed to draw the attention of these spirits or souls, increasing the likelihood of the wish being granted.

3. Symbolic Representation of Transformation:

Shooting stars are transient and ephemeral, appearing suddenly and disappearing quickly. This fleeting nature has led to associations with transformation and change. Seeing a shooting star may symbolize a moment of opportunity or a turning point in one's life. Making a wish on a shooting star is seen as a way to harness that transformative energy and manifest positive changes or desires in one's life.

It's important to note that the belief in shooting stars granting wishes is rooted in superstition and symbolism rather than any empirical evidence. Nonetheless, the sight of a shooting star continues to captivate the imagination of many people, and the act of making a wish upon one remains a cherished tradition associated with hope, dreams, and the possibility of something magical coming true.

Horseshoes

"Horseshoes are thought to bring good luck. They should be hung with the ends pointing up to prevent the good luck from "running out". "

Curse of the horseshoe

The quiet town of Salem Hollow had never known anything more complex or sinister than the occasional livestock theft until the day Luke Brenner moved in. Brenner was a blacksmith by trade, a big, burly man with a penetrating gaze. He had a reputation for his fine craftsmanship, especially his horseshoes, which were sought after by horse owners near and far.

Luke's life was simple, but in his heart, he harbored a deep resentment. A bitter feud had driven him from his previous town, and he blamed the community for his misfortune. In an act of revenge, he crafted a special horseshoe, pouring all his rage and bitterness into the red-hot iron.

As he worked, he whispered an ancient curse he'd learned from his grandmother, a woman rumored to be a witch. He infused this horseshoe with malice, intending it to bring misfortune to anyone who used it.

The cursed horseshoe was beautiful, polished to a high shine, and etched with intricate designs. It was a masterpiece, and Luke knew just the person to gift it to - Mayor Alden, the wealthiest man in Salem Hollow, and a proud owner of a fine stallion.

Mayor Alden was thrilled with the gift. He had the horseshoe fitted to his stallion right away, unaware of the curse that had been bestowed upon it.

The misfortunes started subtly. Mayor Alden's stallion, once a champion racer, began losing races. Then, the horse fell sick. Veterinarians were baffled as the stallion's health continued to deteriorate despite their best efforts. And then, Mayor Alden himself fell ill. Doctors were called from all around, but none could diagnose his ailment.

The tragedies didn't stop with Mayor Alden. His illness seemed to spread like a plague, infecting the town. Crops failed, livestock died, and people fell ill. Panic swept through Salem Hollow as its residents searched for the source of their misfortune.

Luke, watching from a distance, was satisfied with his revenge. The town was suffering just as he had suffered. But his satisfaction turned to horror when he saw the extent of the damage. He hadn't intended for this. The curse was too powerful, too destructive.

Racked with guilt, he decided to confess and right his wrongs. He revealed the cursed horseshoe to the town and admitted his vengeful act. The town's people were in uproar. They demanded justice, but Luke offered a solution instead. He would craft a horseshoe of protection to counteract the curse.

Working day and night, Luke poured his regret and hope into the new horseshoe. His intentions were pure, but the town was skeptical. They had been burned once, and their trust was not easily regained.

When the horseshoe was ready, Luke personally fit it onto Mayor Alden's stallion. The horse, now a skeletal shadow of its former self, stood still, seemingly aware of the importance of the moment.

Slowly, the stallion's health began to improve. The crops started to regain their vitality, and the townsfolk started to recover. It was a slow process, but the town of Salem Hollow was healing.

Luke, however, was not forgiven. He was exiled from Salem Hollow, forced to wander and find a new home. But he left with a heavy heart and a newfound understanding of the power he wielded.

In his journey, he became a story, a fable told to children. The tale of the blacksmith who, in his quest for revenge, nearly destroyed a town. A story of power, revenge, and redemption.

The story of the cursed horseshoe. The story of
Luke Brenner.

**Now let's break down this superstition of the
horseshoe:**

The superstition surrounding horseshoes as
symbols of good luck dates back to ancient
times and is rooted in a number of cultures and
traditions.

One of the most popular narratives comes from
a Christian legend about St. Dunstan, who was
a blacksmith before becoming the Archbishop
of Canterbury in the 10th century.

According to the legend, the Devil visited St.
Dunstan and asked him to shoe his horse. St.
Dunstan recognized the Devil and tricked him.
He nailed a horseshoe to the Devil's foot
instead of his horse. The Devil experienced
intense pain, and St. Dunstan agreed to remove
the shoe only after making the Devil promise
never to enter a place where a horseshoe is

hung above the door. This is one explanation for why horseshoes are considered lucky and are often hung above doorways.

The horseshoe's shape also has significance. Its crescent form is similar to the moon's, which has been a symbol of fertility and good fortune in many cultures.

As for hanging the horseshoe with the ends pointing up, this is said to keep the good luck from "running out." The idea is that the horseshoe acts like a little storage container for good fortune. If it's hung with the ends pointing down, the good luck is said to pour out. Conversely, if it's hung with the ends pointing up, it's said to collect good luck and bring prosperity to those living in or entering the home.

In a more practical sense, horseshoes were traditionally made of iron, a material that was believed to ward off evil spirits in many cultures. In addition, the process of making a horseshoe involves fire and hammering, which can be seen as powerful and transformative forces, enhancing the horseshoe's protective qualities.

Beyond these specific beliefs, horseshoes are often associated more generally with horses, which have traditionally been seen as symbols of strength, power, and dependability in many cultures. Thus, a horseshoe might also be seen as bringing with it the positive attributes of the horse itself.

Touching Red

"In some parts of the United Kingdom, upon hearing the first cuckoo of the spring, one must touch something red to ensure good luck for the rest of the year."

The red scarf

The town of Harrows End was a quaint place, nestled between rolling hills and dense forests. Its people were kind and superstitious, and one of their most peculiar beliefs was that touching something red would ward off bad luck. Lacey Donovan, a freelance journalist, had recently moved to Harrows End. Intrigued by the town's unique beliefs and traditions, Lacey decided to participate in this ritual.

She bought a red silk scarf from a local boutique. It was a vibrant, deep red, the kind that seemed to shimmer under the light. The moment she touched it, a chill ran down her spine, but she dismissed it as the thrill of indulging in the town's superstition.

That night, Lacey had her first nightmare. She found herself in a realm of red, a place where the air was thick with a sense of impending doom. A shadowy figure lurked in the corner of her vision, always out of focus, always watching. She woke up in a cold sweat, her heart pounding in her chest. She chalked it up to stress and tried to forget about it.

However, the nightmares persisted. Every night, the figure in the dream came closer, growing more menacing. And then, strange things started happening in her waking life. She would see flashes of red out of the corner of her eye, hear whispers in her ear. She felt a growing dread, an unshakeable feeling of being watched.

When she talked to the townsfolk about it, they became worried. They had never heard of such occurrences. They believed that red was a protector, not a tormentor. The town's elder, a woman named Agnes, seemed particularly disturbed. She asked Lacey about the red object she had touched, and upon seeing the red scarf, her face turned ashen.

Agnes revealed that the scarf had belonged to a woman who was believed to be a witch. The woman had been banished from the town years ago after she was accused of inviting a malevolent entity into our world. She had used the color red as a conduit, and the scarf was one of her belongings that had been left behind.

Lacey was filled with horror. She had unknowingly invited a malevolent entity into her life, and it was feeding on her fear and despair. She had to do something.

Agnes suggested a ritual to banish the entity. It was risky and required Lacey to face her fear, but it was the only way. Lacey agreed, determined to take back control of her life.

The ritual was held at midnight, under a new moon. Lacey, with the red scarf in hand, stood in the town's center, surrounded by its people. As Agnes chanted in a language Lacey didn't understand, she felt a presence. The air turned cold, and she could see her breath fogging up despite it being summer.

Suddenly, the entity appeared. It was a terrifying, shadowy figure, just like in her dreams. Lacey felt a wave of fear wash over her, but she stood her ground. She held up the red scarf, and with a voice louder than she thought she could muster, she commanded the entity to leave and never return.

For a moment, nothing happened. Then, the entity shrieked, a bone-chilling sound that made everyone wince. The red of the scarf seemed to glow brighter for a moment, then faded away, taking the entity with it.

With the entity gone, Lacey felt a sense of relief wash over her. The townsfolk cheered, their beliefs in the protective power of red slightly shaken but not shattered.

Lacey's life returned to normal, but she was changed. She had faced her fears and come out stronger. The town of Harrows End had a new story to tell, a tale of a brave woman named

Lacey Donovan, who banished an evil entity with a red scarf and her courage.

Her story served as a reminder to the town and to herself that fear could invite darkness, but courage could banish it. And the color red, once a symbol of protection, was now a symbol of bravery and strength in Harrows End, thanks to Lacey.

Now let's break down this superstition of touching red:

1.United Kingdom:
The tradition of "touching red" upon hearing the first cuckoo of spring in the United Kingdom is a more localized and specific superstition, and its origins are not as widely documented or understood as some other superstitions. However, it's generally believed to be rooted in the symbolism associated with cuckoos and the color red.

2.European Culture:

Cuckoos are often associated with the arrival of spring and the renewal of life, as they tend to make their distinctive call when they return to the UK and other parts of Europe after spending the winter in warmer climates. This has led to many traditions and superstitions related to cuckoos, with their call often being seen as a harbinger of good luck.

3.Chinese Culture:
The act of touching something red could be related to the symbolism of the color red in many cultures. Red is often associated with good luck, protection, and warding off evil. For example, in Chinese culture, red is the color of good luck and is used in nearly all traditional celebrations.

By combining these two symbols, this superstition suggests that touching something red upon hearing the first cuckoo of the spring could amplify the good luck associated with the cuckoo's call. It's a way of acknowledging and welcoming the positive energy brought by the arrival of spring, and of actively participating in the renewal of life that it represents.

However, it's important to note that superstitions can vary significantly even within a single country or culture, and the specific beliefs and practices associated with them can be influenced by many factors. They can evolve over time and can be interpreted in different ways by different people. This makes them a fascinating aspect of cultural heritage, but also means that their origins and meanings can sometimes be difficult to trace with certainty.

Avoiding the Number 13

"In many Western cultures, the number 13 is considered unlucky. This is why some buildings skip the 13th floor or hotels lack a room number 13."

The 13th floor

Luna Carter was a fiercely independent young woman with a penchant for adventure. When she moved to the bustling city of New York, she found excitement in the prospect of living in a high-rise apartment. However, her enthusiasm dimmed when she discovered that the only available unit was on the 13th floor of a building with a dark history. Despite her unease, Luna was determined to make the best of her new home.

Upon settling in, Luna was quick to notice the peculiar atmosphere that permeated the 13th floor. The hallway seemed unnaturally dim, and a chill hung in the air even on the warmest days. Strange sounds echoed through the halls at night, and Luna often caught glimpses of movement out of the corner of her eye, only to find nothing there when she turned to look.

As the weeks passed, Luna's unease grew into a gnawing fear. She began to experience increasingly bizarre phenomena. Objects would inexplicably move or disappear, and she would hear whispers that seemed to emanate from the very walls of her apartment. The number 13 seemed to haunt her at every turn, appearing in unexpected places and taking on an ominous significance.

Driven by a growing sense of dread, Luna delved into the building's history, uncovering a dark tale of tragedy and misfortune. Decades ago, a series of unexplained deaths had occurred on the 13th floor, and rumors circulated about a malevolent presence that had terrorized the building's residents. The floor had been abandoned for years before being reopened to tenants, but the specter of its troubled past lingered.

Determined to unravel the mysteries of the 13th floor, Luna delved deeper into her investigation, seeking out former residents and scouring old records. She learned of a young woman named Evelyn, who had been at the center of the tragic events that had plagued the floor. Rumors suggested that Evelyn had dabbled in the occult and had summoned a dark force that had wrought havoc on the building.

As Luna pieced together the fragments of the past, the paranormal phenomena escalated. She found herself plagued by vivid nightmares and waking visions that left her shaken and disoriented. She became convinced that the malevolent force that had haunted the 13th floor was now targeting her, seeking to draw her into its web of despair and madness.

In a desperate bid to protect herself, Luna sought out a reclusive occult scholar who had once investigated the building's dark history. The scholar spoke of ancient rituals and protective charms, warning Luna that she was treading on dangerous ground. Nevertheless, he offered her guidance, providing her with

talismans and incantations that might shield her
from the malevolent force.

Armed with the scholar's knowledge, Luna
embarked on a perilous journey to confront the
darkness that lurked within the 13th floor.
Armed with protective symbols and a heart
filled with determination, Luna faced the
malevolent force that had tormented her.

In a climactic confrontation, Luna invoked the
ancient incantations and wielded the protective
talismans, challenging the malevolent force to
release its grip on her and the building. As she
stood her ground, a powerful surge of energy
filled the air, and the shadows that had plagued
her began to dissipate.

In the aftermath of the confrontation, Luna felt
a profound sense of relief wash over her. The
oppressive atmosphere that had hung over the
13th floor lifted, and the apartment building
was filled with an eerie calm. The whispers and
shadows that had haunted Luna's days and
nights were gone, replaced by a newfound
sense of peace.

With the malevolent force banished, Luna found closure in the mysteries she had unraveled. The building's dark history, once a source of fear and uncertainty, had been laid to rest. Luna's courage and determination had not only saved herself but had also brought an end to the 13th floor's troubled past.

As time passed, the 13th floor became just another part of the building, its dark history fading into memory. Luna, too, found peace, knowing that she had faced the unknown and emerged triumphant. Her story became a whispered legend among the building's residents, a tale of bravery and resilience in the face of darkness.

Luna's experience taught her that sometimes, confronting the unknown was the only way to find peace. Her journey on the 13th floor had been a harrowing one, but it had also been a transformative one. She emerged stronger, with a newfound understanding of the power of courage and resilience.

The building's dark history became a cautionary tale, a reminder that some secrets are best left undisturbed. Luna, however, knew that the truth had set her free. She had faced the malevolent force that had haunted the 13th floor, and in doing so, had found the strength to overcome her deepest fears.

The 13th floor remained a part of Luna's past, but it also became a symbol of her unwavering determination and resilience. Her experience had taught her that even in the face of the unknown, one could find the strength to survive and thrive.

As Luna moved forward, she carried with her the lessons she had learned on the 13th floor. She knew that she had confronted true darkness and emerged victorious, and that knowledge would always be a source of strength in the face of life's uncertainties.

From that day forward, Luna embraced each new challenge with a fearless spirit, knowing that she had faced the malevolent force that lurked in the shadows and had emerged stronger for it. Her journey on the 13th floor had become a testament to the power of resilience and the triumph of the human spirit over darkness.

Now let's break down this superstition of avoiding the number 13:

The superstition surrounding the number 13, particularly in Western cultures, has a few potential origins rooted in religion, mythology, and history.

One of the most common theories relates to Christianity. At the Last Supper, there were 13 individuals present: Jesus Christ and his 12 apostles. Judas, who is often counted as the 13th guest, is the apostle who betrayed Jesus, leading to His crucifixion. Subsequently, 13 came to be viewed as an omen of bad luck due to this association.

Another theory comes from Norse mythology. According to the myth, the god Odin held a banquet in Valhalla for 11 of his closest gods. Loki, the god of mischief and chaos, was not invited but showed up anyway, making the total number of gods present 13. Loki caused the death of Balder, the god of light, joy, and reconciliation, during this gathering. Hence, 13 came to be associated with chaos and misfortune.

Historically, negative associations with the number 13 can also be found in legal systems and cultural practices. For example, in ancient Rome, witches reportedly gathered in groups of 12. The 13th was believed to be the devil.

The fear of the number 13 is so pervasive, it even has a scientific name: triskaidekaphobia. This fear has influenced architecture and design, as seen in buildings that omit the 13th floor or hotels without a room number 13. The Friday the 13th superstition, which is considered an especially unlucky day in Western superstition, is another reflection of this fear.

It's worth noting that not all cultures view the number 13 as unlucky. In some cultures, such as in China, the number 13 is considered lucky because its pronunciation sounds similar to the word for "surely alive" or "definitely vibrant".

Saying " Bless You" When Someone Sneezes

"This originated from the belief that a person's soul could be thrown from their body when they sneezed. Saying "bless you" was a way of keeping the soul safe."

Bless you

Michelle always had a strange peculiarity. It began when she was just a child, a little girl of no more than six. She'd sneeze, and her mother would instinctively say, "Bless you." But with each 'bless you,' Michelle could feel an unnerving sensation, a coldness that crept up her spine and made the hairs on her neck stand on end. But she was just a child, and her fears were dismissed as an overactive imagination.

As she grew older, the sense of dread that accompanied each 'bless you' grew too. It was an unseen weight that bore down on her, a darkness that seemed to surround her. The feeling was so strong that Michelle began to avoid people, fearful of their well-meaning words. She became a recluse, a shell of her former self, living in perpetual anxiety.

One day, she sneezed in her apartment, and the silence that followed was a welcome relief. She was starting to believe that she was safe, that maybe she'd been wrong all along. But then, her phone buzzed. It was a text message from her mother, reading, "Bless you."

The room darkened instantly, even though it was midday. Michelle felt a chill wind rush past her, extinguishing the lights and casting long shadows across her small apartment. She could feel a presence, a dark entity that had been growing stronger with each 'bless you.' She clenched her eyes shut, praying for it to go away, but she could feel it getting closer.

Suddenly, an icy hand gripped her shoulder. The touch was soul-suckingly cold, sapping away her strength. She could feel the entity inside her, consuming her, possessing her. Michelle tried to resist, but it was too strong. It was inside her mind, showing her images of blood, death, and destruction. She screamed, but no sound came out. She was trapped inside her own body, a prisoner to the malevolent force that was now in control.

Days turned into weeks and weeks into months. Michelle was no more. The entity had taken over, using her body as a vessel to cause chaos and wreak havoc. It fed on fear, terrorizing those around her, and growing stronger with each passing day. Michelle's body was deteriorating, but the entity kept her alive, feeding off the energy of those around her.

One day, in a moment of clarity, Michelle found herself back in control. The entity was dormant, resting after a night of unspeakable horror. She was weak, drained of all energy, but she knew she had to fight back. She mustered all the strength she had left and started researching, looking for a way to rid herself of the entity.

She learned of an ancient ritual that required her to confront the entity, to force it to reveal its true name. Once she knew its name, she could banish it forever. The ritual was dangerous, risking not only her life but her soul as well. But she was desperate. She had nothing left to lose.

On a stormy night, when the entity was at its strongest, Michelle began the ritual. Lightning flashed, and thunder roared as she chanted ancient words, calling out to the entity. It woke up, angry and violent, threatening to tear her apart from the inside. But she held on, continuing the ritual despite the excruciating pain.

Finally, she forced the entity to reveal its name. It was a guttural, unholy sound that seemed to echo in the room. Armed with its name, Michelle banished the entity, sending it back to the dark abyss from where it came. The room lightened instantly, and the coldness dissipated. Michelle collapsed, exhausted, but triumphant.

Years later, Michelle still lived in isolation, avoiding people as much as she could. She never sneezed, and on the rare occasion she did, she made sure she was alone. She had survived a nightmare, a horror beyond comprehension. But she was stronger for it, a survivor in the truest sense of the word.

Every time she heard a "Bless you," an icy shiver would run down her spine, a grim reminder of her terrifying past. But she was no longer fearful. She knew the entity's name, and she was ready to face it, to banish it, should it ever return. To the world, she was Michelle, the recluse. But to herself, she was Michelle, the survivor, the woman who had stared into the eyes of a malevolent force and lived to tell the tale.

Now let's break down this superstition of saying " bless you " when someone sneezes:

The practice of saying "bless you" when someone sneezes has a long and varied history, with several different cultural and mythical origins. The idea that a person's soul could be thrown from their body when they sneezed is one of the most commonly cited explanations for the origin of this superstition.

In many ancient cultures, sneezing was often seen as a sign of impending illness or even death. The ancient Greeks, for example, believed that a sneeze was a sign that the soul was leaving the body. In response to this belief, they would say "long life" or "to your health" after someone sneezed, in an effort to keep the soul within the body and to ward off any potential illness or harm.

In various other cultures, similar beliefs and practices surrounding sneezing and the soul exist. For instance, in some cultures, it was believed that a sneeze could open the body to evil spirits, and saying "bless you" was a way of protecting the sneezer from these malevolent forces.

The phrase "bless you" itself has religious origins, as it is often associated with the Christian tradition. It's believed that the practice of saying "God bless you" or "bless you" after a sneeze may have originated in response to the bubonic plague, as sneezing was a symptom of the disease, and a sneeze was often the first sign that someone was infected. In this context, saying "bless you" was a way of invoking divine protection for the sneezer in the face of a potentially deadly illness.

Over time, the practice of saying "bless you" when someone sneezes has become deeply ingrained in many cultures, and it is now often simply considered a polite social convention rather than a response to a specific superstition or belief. Nonetheless, the historical and cultural origins of this practice are rooted in a rich tapestry of beliefs about the body, the soul, and the supernatural.

Carrying a Bride Over the Threshold

"This superstition has a few different origins, but some believe it began with the idea of protecting the bride from evil spirits that might be lurking below the threshold."

The New Bride

Malcolm and Maria were the epitome of young love, blissfully happy and ready to start their new life together. They had just tied the knot, and Malcolm, adhering to the age-old tradition, lifted Maria in his arms to carry her over the threshold of their new home. It was an old, Victorian house with a rich history and an irresistible charm. Little did they know, the house had a dark secret.

As Malcolm crossed the threshold, he felt a sudden chill, as though he had walked into an invisible wall of cold. Maria felt it too; a shiver ran down her spine, but they both shrugged it off as a draft. They were too happy, too excited about their new life to pay it much mind. That was their first mistake.

As the days turned into weeks, Maria started to change. She was no longer the bubbly, vivacious woman Malcolm had fallen in love with. She was distant, cold, and had a temper that would flare up at the smallest provocation. She would spend hours alone in the attic, refusing to let Malcolm in. She claimed she was just unpacking, but Malcolm knew something was wrong. It was as though Maria was a different person, a stranger living in his wife's body.

One night, Malcolm woke up to find Maria's side of the bed empty. He found her in the attic, staring at an old, dusty mirror. He called out to her, but she didn't respond. She just stood there, staring at her reflection. As he looked closer, Malcolm could see a dark figure in the mirror standing behind Maria. He screamed, but Maria didn't react. It was as if she were in a trance.

The figure in the mirror was a woman dressed in a wedding dress, her face hidden under a veil. Malcolm watched in horror as Maria turned around to face the figure. The woman lifted her veil, revealing a face twisted in rage and hatred. Then, she reached out, her hands passing through the mirror to grip Maria's shoulders. Maria screamed, a sound filled with pure terror, and the room plunged into darkness.

When Malcolm woke up, he was in the hospital. The doctors said he'd been found unconscious in the attic. They assumed he had fallen and hit his head, causing him to hallucinate. But Malcolm knew what he had seen was real.

Maria had disappeared. The police searched the house, but there was no sign of her. Malcolm tried to tell them about the figure in the mirror, but they dismissed it as a result of his head injury. They said Maria probably left of her own free will. But Malcolm knew better. He knew Maria was still in the house, trapped in the mirror by the vengeful spirit.

Desperate to save his wife, Malcolm sought the help of a local medium. She told him the house was haunted by a jilted bride who had been left at the altar. Heartbroken, she had hung herself in the attic, vowing to take revenge on any happy bride who crossed the threshold.

To free Maria, Malcolm had to appease the spirit. The medium instructed him to find the bride's lost engagement ring, which was hidden somewhere in the house, and return it to the spirit. The search was grueling, filled with terrifying encounters with the spirit, but Malcolm was determined. He would save Maria, no matter the cost.

Finally, he found the ring hidden in a secret compartment in the attic. As he held it up to the mirror, the vengeful bride appeared. Malcolm could see the pain in her eyes, the desperation for closure. He apologized on behalf of the groom who had abandoned her and offered her the ring.

The bride's face softened, and she reached out to take the ring. As she slipped it onto her finger, she began to fade, her anger and hatred dissipating. Then, Maria appeared in the mirror. She reached out, and Malcolm pulled her out of the mirror and into his arms.

The house was peaceful after that. Malcolm and Maria started their life anew, living in harmony with the spirit. The bride was no longer vengeful, her anger pacified by the return of her ring. She was a silent observer, a reminder of the house's dark history.

Malcolm and Maria learned a valuable lesson that day: every tradition, no matter how innocent, can have unforeseen consequences. But they also learned that love and determination can overcome even the darkest of forces.

Now let's break down this superstition of carrying a bride over the threshold:

The tradition of carrying a bride over the threshold has a range of mythical backstories, origins, and cultural significance, with the belief that it protects the bride from evil spirits being one of the commonly cited explanations.

One of the most prevalent origin stories stems from ancient Roman and European traditions. It was believed that a bride was particularly vulnerable to evil spirits and ill omens at the threshold of her new home. By carrying her over the threshold, the groom was thought to protect her from these malevolent forces, ensuring a prosperous and harmonious beginning to their marriage.

In some cultures, the act of carrying the bride over the threshold symbolized the bride's reluctance to leave her family and the transition into her new life with her husband. By being lifted over the threshold, she was physically and symbolically brought into her new home and future with her husband.

Additionally, in medieval Europe, there was a belief that the bride might be targeted by jealous spirits or envious individuals who sought to curse the couple. Carrying the bride over the threshold was thought to confuse these spirits and prevent them from following the couple into their new home, thereby safeguarding their happiness and union.

In certain cultural interpretations, the act of carrying the bride over the threshold also symbolized the groom's strength, providing a demonstration of his ability to protect and care for his new wife. This act was seen as a gesture of love and commitment, demonstrating the groom's willingness to support and shield his bride from harm.

Throughout history, various superstitions and beliefs have surrounded weddings, and carrying the bride over the threshold is just one example of the many rituals designed to protect the couple and ensure a prosperous and harmonious union. While the practice may have evolved over time and lost some of its original supernatural significance, it remains a cherished tradition in many cultures, symbolizing the beginning of a new chapter in the couple's lives.

Tossing a Coin in a Fountain for Good Luck

"This tradition dates back to ancient Rome where people would throw coins into fountains to appease the gods and bring good fortune."

The Unlucky Fountain

Isabella, Troy, Gabriel, and Nathaniel were a group of adventurous friends who often sought thrills in the unlikeliest of places. One warm summer day, they stumbled upon a forgotten fountain in the heart of an overgrown park. The fountain was adorned with weather-worn statues and filled with shimmering coins, tossed in by visitors seeking good luck. Intrigued, the friends decided to retrieve the coins, unaware of the dark secret that lay hidden beneath the surface.

As they reached into the water to collect the coins, they felt a sudden chill, and the once gentle breeze turned into a howling wind. A sense of unease settled over them, but they dismissed it as a simple case of nerves. However, as they gathered the coins, they began to feel as though they were being watched, a feeling that grew stronger with each handful of treasure they retrieved.

Suddenly, the water began to churn, and a twisted, shadowy figure emerged from the depths of the fountain. It was the guardian of the coins, a malevolent creature that had been bound to the fountain for centuries. Its eyes burned with a fierce, otherworldly light, and its twisted form filled the friends' hearts with terror.

The creature spoke in a voice that seemed to echo from the depths of the earth, warning the friends to leave its treasure be. But they were determined to keep the coins they had collected. In a fit of rage, the creature lunged at them, its claws slashing through the air with terrifying speed.

Isabella, Troy, Gabriel, and Nathaniel ran for their lives, the guardian hot on their heels. They knew they had awakened something ancient and powerful, and they were ill-prepared for the battle that lay ahead.

They sought refuge in the park's abandoned conservatory, a place long forgotten by the townspeople. As they caught their breath, they realized that they were trapped. The guardian prowled outside, its piercing gaze fixed on the building, waiting for the perfect opportunity to strike.

As night fell, the friends worked together to devise a plan. They knew they had to confront the creature to stand a chance at surviving. Armed with makeshift weapons and a newfound determination, they ventured out into the darkness, ready to face the guardian.

The battle that ensued was unlike anything they had ever experienced. The creature unleashed a barrage of dark magic, forcing the friends to fight for their lives. It was a harrowing struggle, filled with fear and desperation, but they refused to back down.

In the heart of the conflict, Isabella discovered an ancient talisman hidden among the coins they had collected. As she clutched the talisman, a surge of power coursed through her, imbuing her with the strength to stand against the guardian. With the talisman in hand, Isabella faced the creature, calling upon its ancient magic to bind the guardian once more.

The guardian let out a deafening roar as the ancient magic took hold, and its form began to fade, dissolving into the night. The friends had emerged victorious, but the price had been steep. They had faced a force beyond their understanding and come out forever changed.

As they gathered the remaining coins, they knew they had been fortunate to survive. The guardian had been vanquished, but the memory of their terrifying encounter would stay with them forever. From that day forward, they understood the true cost of seeking good luck in forgotten places, and they knew they had been forever changed.

As they gathered the remaining coins, they knew they had been fortunate to survive. The guardian had been vanquished, but the memory of their terrifying encounter would stay with them forever. From that day forward, they understood the true cost of seeking good luck in forgotten places, and they knew they had to be careful when delving into the unknown.

Leaving the park behind, the friends made a solemn vow never to speak of the events that had transpired that fateful day. They knew that the world was filled with ancient guardians and long-forgotten spirits, and they had no desire to attract more unwanted attention.

As time passed, the friends grew closer, bound by the harrowing experience they had shared. The talisman that Isabella had found remained a symbol of their resilience and unity, a reminder of the strength they had discovered within themselves.

Though they had faced unimaginable danger, the friends emerged from the ordeal with a newfound respect for the mysteries of the world. Their bond had been tested, and they had prevailed. They understood that the pursuit of good luck could come at a great cost, and they were content to cherish the simple blessings that life bestowed upon them each day.

In the end, the friends emerged from the shadows of the forgotten fountain as survivors, forever changed by their encounter with the guardian. They carried with them the knowledge that sometimes, the pursuit of good luck could lead to unforeseen consequences, and they vowed to approach life's mysteries with caution and reverence.

As they looked to the future, they knew that they would always carry the memory of that day with them. The guardian had been vanquished, but the echoes of its malevolent presence would linger in their minds, a reminder of the price they had paid for venturing into the realm of the unknown. And though they would never forget the darkness they had faced, they also knew that they had emerged from it stronger, bound together by an unbreakable bond forged in the fires of their shared ordeal.

Now let's break down this superstition of tossing a coin in a fountain for good luck:

The tradition of tossing a coin into a fountain for good luck indeed has a rich and varied historical background, with its origins often traced back to ancient Rome and the belief in appeasing the gods for good fortune.

In ancient Rome, throwing coins into fountains and other bodies of water was a common practice associated with various beliefs and rituals. Water was considered a sacred element, often linked to divine powers and spiritual significance. Fountains and natural springs were regarded as places where the divine and earthly realms intersected, making them ideal locations for making offerings to the gods.

The act of tossing a coin into a fountain was seen as a gesture of respect and tribute to the water deities, as well as a way to seek their favor and blessings. It was believed that by making these offerings, individuals could gain the goodwill of the gods and goddesses associated with water, ensuring their protection, prosperity, and good fortune.

Furthermore, there was a widespread belief in the concept of "wishing wells" or "lucky wells" in many cultures, where people would throw coins or other offerings into wells, springs, or fountains while making a wish. The belief was that the act of making a wish and offering a token to the water spirits or deities would increase the likelihood of the wish being granted.

Over time, the tradition of tossing coins into fountains for good luck has evolved and become a popular practice in various parts of the world, often associated with tourist attractions and iconic landmarks. While the original religious and supernatural significance may have faded, the act of making a wish and tossing a coin into a fountain remains a cherished tradition, symbolizing hope, good fortune, and the fulfillment of desires.

Today, the practice of tossing coins into fountains continues to be embraced as a lighthearted and whimsical gesture, with many people participating in the tradition as a fun and symbolic way to express their hopes and aspirations for the future.

Wishbones

"It is believed that whoever breaks the wishbone and has the larger piece will have their wish come true."

Wish Upon a Wishbone

Marie and Renae were always inseparable. The two sisters had grown up exploring the woods near their family's cabin, and on one fateful autumn day, they stumbled upon a hidden cave deep in the heart of the forest. Intrigued, they ventured inside, their footsteps echoing off the damp walls.

As they delved deeper into the cave, the air grew colder, and a sense of unease settled over them. The sisters pressed on, their curiosity driving them forward until they arrived at a vast chamber bathed in an eerie blue light. In the center of the chamber lay a massive wishbone, its surface glistening with an otherworldly sheen.

Renae's eyes widened with excitement. "Look, Marie! It's a wishbone! Let's make a wish and break it!"

Marie hesitated, feeling a sense of foreboding, but Renae was already reaching for the wishbone. With a swift motion, she snapped it in two, and a chill wind filled the chamber, extinguishing their lanterns and plunging them into darkness.

A bone-chilling cackle echoed through the cave, freezing the sisters in their tracks. Suddenly, the chamber was alight with an unearthly glow, and before them stood a spectral figure cloaked in tattered robes—the long-dead witch whose resting place they had disturbed.

"Who dares to awaken me from my slumber?" the witch hissed, her voice a twisted melody of malice and hatred.

Trembling with fear, Marie stammered, "We didn't mean to disturb you. We—"

But before she could finish, the witch's piercing gaze fell upon them, and with a wave of her bony hand, she sent them hurtling into the darkness.

When the sisters awoke, they found themselves outside the cave, disoriented and shaken. As they made their way back to the cabin, they couldn't shake the feeling of being watched, and strange occurrences began to plague them. Objects moved on their own, whispers echoed through the halls at night, and an unshakable sense of dread hung in the air.

Desperate for answers, Marie and Renae sought the help of an elderly woman rumored to be well-versed in the supernatural. The woman's name was Eliza, and she lived on the outskirts of the forest in a small, secluded cottage.

Eliza listened intently as the sisters recounted their harrowing experience, her eyes darkening with concern. "You have awakened a powerful curse," she said gravely. "The witch seeks revenge on those who disturbed her resting place, and she will stop at nothing to claim your souls."

Determined to help the sisters, Eliza delved into ancient tomes and whispered incantations, searching for a way to break the curse. But the witch's malevolent presence grew stronger with each passing day, and soon, the forest itself seemed to conspire against them.

One moonlit night, as the sisters huddled together in their cabin, a bloodcurdling scream pierced the silence. Rushing outside, they found Eliza's cottage engulfed in flames, the flickering light casting twisted shadows upon the trees.

With tears in her eyes, Eliza emerged from the inferno, her face etched with sorrow. "The witch is relentless," she said, her voice heavy with resignation. "There is only one way to break the curse. You must find the witch's earthly remains and lay her spirit to rest once and for all."

The sisters nodded, their resolve steeled by Eliza's words. With Eliza's guidance, they embarked on a perilous journey through the heart of the forest, following cryptic clues that led them to long-forgotten landmarks and hidden passages.

As they ventured deeper into the woods, the witch's influence grew more palpable, twisting the very fabric of nature itself. Trees contorted into grotesque shapes, and the air thrummed with an unnatural energy, but the sisters pressed on, driven by the hope of breaking the curse.

Finally, guided by an ancient map, they discovered a desolate clearing where a gnarled oak stood sentinel over a weathered gravestone. As they brushed away the moss and lichen, they uncovered the name of the witch—Evelyn Blackwood—and beneath it, the date of her demise.

With trembling hands, they began to dig, unearthing the witch's skeletal remains. As the first rays of dawn pierced the darkness, they laid her bones to rest, whispering a solemn prayer for peace.

But as the last shovel of earth fell upon the grave, a bone-chilling wail echoed through the forest, and the ground trembled beneath their feet. The witch's ghost materialized before them, her eyes blazing with fury.

"You thought you could defeat me?" she hissed, her voice a cacophony of rage. "You have unleashed forces beyond your comprehension."

The earth convulsed, and tendrils of darkness snaked from the ground, ensnaring the sisters in a suffocating grip. Desperate, they reached for the amulets Eliza had given them, the only hope against the witch's vengeful spirit. With a surge of willpower, they channeled the amulets' power, and a blinding light erupted from the charms, repelling the witch's malevolent grasp.

The forest fell silent, the oppressive aura of malevolence dissipating like morning mist. The witch's ghost let out a final, agonized shriek before vanishing into the ether, her curse broken at last.

Exhausted but victorious, the sisters emerged from the forest, the weight of the curse lifted from their shoulders. The sun bathed the world in a warm glow, and as they made their way back to the cabin, a sense of peace settled over the land.

In the days that followed, the forest began to bloom anew, its once-twisted boughs reaching for the sky with renewed vitality. As for Marie and Renae, they carried the memory of their harrowing ordeal, forever bound by the unbreakable bond of sisterhood and the knowledge that some secrets are better left undisturbed.

From that day forward, they continued to explore the woods, but they never ventured near the hidden cave again, content to leave its dark secrets undisturbed. And as the years passed, the tale of the witch of the forest became a cautionary legend, a reminder of the perils that lurked in the shadows and the enduring strength of those who dared to face them.

Now let's break down this superstition of the wishbone:

The tradition of breaking wishbones, often associated with the custom of making a wish, has a historical basis in folklore and superstition.

The origin of the wishbone tradition can be traced back to ancient European cultures, particularly the practice of divination and seeking good fortune. The tradition is believed to have its roots in the ancient Etruscans and Romans, who would dry and save the wishbone from a cooked bird, usually a chicken, as a token of good luck.

The act of breaking the wishbone was a ritualistic practice that involved two people each taking hold of one end of the bone and pulling it apart. The person who ended up with the larger piece was believed to be granted good luck and the fulfillment of a wish.

The association of the wishbone with luck and wish fulfillment is linked to the idea of avian or bird symbolism in ancient cultures. Birds were often seen as messengers of the divine and were associated with good fortune, making the wishbone a potent symbol of luck and auspiciousness.

In some traditions, the wishbone was also seen as a way to access the wisdom of the birds. The V-shaped fork of the wishbone was thought to resemble the letter "Y," symbolizing the diverging paths of fate or the duality of choices. As such, breaking the wishbone was not only a means of seeking good fortune but also a form of divination, with the resulting split indicating the direction that fate might take.

Over time, the tradition of breaking wishbones has become a lighthearted and playful custom, often associated with celebratory meals, particularly during Thanksgiving. While the original superstitions and symbolic meanings may have evolved or diminished, the act of making a wish and breaking the wishbone remains a cherished tradition, symbolizing hope, optimism, and the pursuit of one's desires.

Avoiding Walking on Cracks

"The saying "step on a crack, break your mother's back" has been a common superstition, encouraging people to avoid stepping on cracks in the sidewalk or road."

The Cracked Sidewalk

Alex was a curious and imaginative child who loved to explore the world around him. One sunny afternoon, while walking home from school, he discovered an old, cracked sidewalk that wound its way through the neighborhood. As he walked, he noticed something peculiar—whenever he stepped on a crack, a faint shimmering light seemed to ripple through the air, as if the very fabric of reality was being distorted.

Intrigued, Alex experimented with his discovery, tentatively stepping on another crack. To his amazement, the shimmering light grew brighter, and before his eyes, a dark, swirling portal materialized, exuding an ominous aura that sent shivers down his spine.

As he peered into the depths of the portal, he caught a glimpse of a sinister parallel world—a place of darkness and malevolence, where grotesque, shadowy figures lurked just beyond the threshold. Horrified, Alex stumbled back, his heart racing with fear.

Determined to understand the nature of these portals, Alex cautiously continued his experiments, and with each step on a crack, the portals grew larger and more numerous, their insidious influence seeping into his world.

Soon, strange occurrences began to plague the neighborhood. Pets vanished without a trace, and eerie whispers echoed through the streets at night. Alex's neighbors grew increasingly fearful, their once-cheerful faces etched with worry and paranoia.

Realizing the dire consequences of his actions, Alex sought the help of his older sister, Emily, a brilliant and resourceful young woman with a keen interest in the supernatural. Together, they delved into ancient tomes and whispered legends, desperate to find a way to close the portals and banish the malevolent creatures that threatened their reality.

As they pieced together fragments of forgotten lore, they learned that the portals were a gateway to a realm of pure darkness, a place where malevolent entities hungered for entry into the world of light. The only way to seal the portals was to find the source of their power and destroy it.

Armed with this knowledge, Alex and Emily embarked on a perilous journey, navigating the treacherous pathways of the parallel world, where the very air seemed to pulse with malice. They encountered grotesque creatures that slithered through the shadows, their eyes gleaming with predatory hunger, and the very fabric of reality seemed to warp and twist around them.

As they ventured deeper into the heart of this malevolent realm, they discovered a towering obelisk pulsating with dark energy—the source of the portals. With a sense of trepidation, they approached the obelisk, determined to put an end to the nightmare that had befallen their world.

As they prepared to destroy the obelisk, the ground trembled, and a horde of malevolent creatures descended upon them, their twisted forms converging in a nightmarish frenzy. With every ounce of courage they could muster, Alex and Emily fought back, wielding ancient artifacts and incantations passed down through generations.

In a blinding flash of light, the obelisk shattered, and the portals collapsed in on themselves, sealing the malevolent creatures within their dark domain once and for all.

As they emerged from the parallel world, the sun bathed their world in a warm glow, and a sense of peace settled over the neighborhood.

Now let's break down this superstition of avoiding walking on cracks:

The superstition of avoiding walking on cracks, often accompanied by the saying "step on a crack, break your mother's back," is a widely recognized belief with various cultural and mythical origins.

The origins of this superstition are not entirely clear, but it has been a part of folklore in Western cultures for many years. It is often associated with childhood games and rhymes, and the saying itself is thought to have originated as a playful warning to encourage children to be mindful of their steps.

One possible explanation for the superstition is rooted in the concept of sympathetic magic, a belief that actions performed on one object can influence another object that is symbolically connected. In this context, stepping on a crack may have been seen as a symbolic act that could bring harm to one's mother, creating a sense of caution and an incentive to avoid such actions.

Additionally, the superstition may have connections to broader beliefs about patterns and omens. In some cultures, patterns and repetitions are believed to hold significance, and stepping on a crack may have been seen as disrupting a natural order or inviting bad luck.

The superstition might also be related to the general concept of avoiding potential sources of harm. In the past, uneven or cracked surfaces could pose a tripping hazard, and the superstition may have served as a mnemonic device to encourage people, especially children, to watch their step and avoid accidents.

While the specific origin of the superstition is not definitively known, the saying and the associated belief in avoiding walking on cracks have persisted over time, becoming a familiar part of popular culture. Many people continue to playfully observe this superstition, often without necessarily believing in its literal consequences, as it has become a lighthearted and whimsical tradition associated with childhood games and nostalgia.

Itchy Palms

"In some cultures, if your right palm itches, you will receive money soon, but an itchy left palm means you'll be losing money soon."

Case of the Itchy Palm

Iris had always been a struggling artist. Her days were filled with endless hours in her dimly lit studio, where she poured her heart and soul into her paintings. But no matter how hard she worked, success eluded her. That was until one eerie night when everything changed.

It started with a subtle itch in the palms of her hands. At first, Iris dismissed it as nothing more than a minor irritation, but as the days passed, the sensation grew more intense. The itching became so unbearable that it kept her up at night, causing her to lose precious hours of sleep.

Desperate for relief, Iris sought out doctors and specialists, but none could provide an explanation or a remedy for her affliction. She felt as if invisible claws were raking across the tender skin of her palms, and no amount of scratching could soothe the maddening itch.

One fateful evening, as Iris sat in her studio, her hands throbbing with discomfort, she felt an overwhelming urge to pick up her paintbrush. Almost involuntarily, she dipped it into a pot of midnight-black paint and began to create. It was as if an unseen force guided her every stroke, and before long, a hauntingly beautiful image emerged on the canvas. The image seemed to pulsate with an otherworldly energy, and as Iris gazed upon it, she felt a chill creep down her spine.

To her surprise, the painting garnered immense attention when she displayed it at a local art exhibition. Critics hailed it as a masterpiece, and collectors clamored to purchase it at exorbitant prices. Iris found herself thrust into the spotlight, her once-empty bank account now overflowing with wealth and opportunity. Yet, with every stroke of her brush, the itching in her palms intensified, as if demanding more of her.

As her fame and fortune grew, so did the darkness that loomed over her. Iris began to notice strange occurrences around her. Shadows seemed to linger where they shouldn't, and whispers echoed in the corners of her mind. She became increasingly paranoid, unable to shake the feeling that something sinister was watching her every move.

One particularly stormy night, as Iris toiled away in her studio, a sudden gust of wind blew out all the candles, plunging the room into darkness. A bone-chilling voice filled the air, its words echoing with a haunting resonance. "Iris," it hissed, "you have benefitted from our pact, but now it is time to pay the price."

Terror seized her heart as she realized the truth. The source of her newfound talent was no mere coincidence—it was a dark pact she had unwittingly made. In exchange for her artistic prowess, she had unknowingly struck a deal with a malevolent entity, and now it had come to claim its due.

With trembling hands, Iris fumbled for a match and lit a single candle, casting a feeble glow across the room. There, in the dim light, she saw a figure materialize before her, its form obscured by the swirling shadows. The entity spoke to her, its voice like a chorus of tormented souls, promising unimaginable power in exchange for her soul.

Refusing to succumb to fear, Iris confronted the entity, demanding to know the true nature of their pact. As the room filled with a palpable sense of dread, the entity revealed its insidious intentions. It sought to consume her soul, to feed on her life force until there was nothing left but an empty husk. In a moment of pure terror, Iris realized the dire consequences of her blind ambition.

Refusing to surrender to the entity's ominous demands, Iris gathered her courage and challenged the sinister being. With a steely resolve, she demanded to renegotiate the terms of their pact, offering an alternative bargain that would spare her soul.

The entity, taken aback by her audacity, considered her proposal. After what felt like an eternity, it spoke again, its voice a chilling whisper in the darkness. It offered her a chance to free herself from the pact, but only if she could create a new masterpiece that surpassed all her previous works. If she failed, her soul would be forfeit, and the entity would claim its prize.

Determined to break free from the clutches of the otherworldly force, Iris accepted the challenge. She poured every ounce of her being into her art, drawing inspiration from the depths of her soul. Day and night blurred together as she feverishly worked, her hands moving with a frantic energy fueled by desperation.

As the deadline approached, Iris put the finishing touches on her magnum opus. The painting was a haunting reflection of her inner turmoil, a visceral portrayal of the torment she had endured. With a trembling hand, she signed her name in the corner, a silent plea woven into every brushstroke.

On the night of the reckoning, Iris presented her creation to the entity, a sense of defiance burning in her eyes. The room filled with an oppressive silence as the entity observed the painting, its unfathomable gaze lingering on the canvas.

Finally, it spoke, its voice tinged with begrudging respect. The entity acknowledged the raw emotion and sheer power imbued in Iris's work, admitting that it surpassed even its own expectations. True to its word, the entity released her from their pact, vanishing into the shadows with a promise never to cross paths with her again.

As the weight of the entity's influence lifted from her life, Iris felt a profound sense of relief wash over her. She knew that the darkness would always linger at the edges of her reality, but she had emerged victorious, her spirit unbroken.

In the aftermath of her harrowing ordeal, Iris returned to her art with a newfound sense of purpose. She channeled her experiences into her creations, infusing them with a depth and emotion that resonated with audiences on a profound level. Her work, born from the crucible of her darkest hour, spoke to the human experience in ways that transcended the boundaries of the tangible world.

Though the memory of the entity's chilling presence lingered in the recesses of her mind, Iris found solace in the knowledge that she had triumphed over the forces that sought to consume her. She continued to create, using her art to exorcise the lingering shadows of her past, and in doing so, she discovered a strength within herself that she never knew she possessed.

As the years passed, Iris's name became synonymous with artistic brilliance, her legacy enduring long after she had departed from this world. Her story lived on as a cautionary tale, a testament to the indomitable spirit of those who dared to confront the darkness within and emerge victorious. And though her hands bore the lingering scars of her ordeal, they also carried the mark of a survivor, a testament to her unwavering resolve in the face of unspeak

Now let's break down this superstition of itchy palms:

The belief surrounding itchy palms, particularly the association of an itchy right palm with the expectation of receiving money and an itchy left palm with the fear of losing money, is a superstition that has been embraced in various cultures and is often linked to folklore and traditional beliefs about luck and fortune.

The superstition has been a part of cultural traditions in different regions for many years, and its specific origins are not definitively known. However, it reflects broader beliefs about the body as a source of signs and omens, and it is often associated with the idea that bodily sensations can be interpreted as indicators of future events.

One potential explanation for the superstition is rooted in the concept of sympathetic magic, which suggests that certain actions or occurrences can influence future events through a symbolic connection. In this context, the sensation of itchiness in the palm might have been seen as a physical manifestation of impending fortune or misfortune, leading to the association with financial gain or loss.

Additionally, the superstition may be connected to broader beliefs about the body as a source of intuitive knowledge. In many cultures, bodily sensations and experiences are believed to hold symbolic meanings, and interpretations of these signs can vary widely based on cultural traditions and local folklore.

It's important to note that the belief in itchy palms and its association with financial outcomes is primarily a superstition and has no scientific basis. Nonetheless, the superstition has persisted over time and continues to be embraced in various cultural contexts as a playful and lighthearted belief, often serving as a topic of casual conversation and a source of amusement.

About the Author

   Porsha Garrett- My love affair with writing began at a tender age, around 10 years old, when I discovered the captivating allure of crafting stories. Armed with my typewriter, I embarked on a journey of creativity, weaving tales that danced with the darkness of the human psyche. It was during this time that I found solace in the works of R.L. Stine and Christopher Pike, masterful authors who effortlessly wove webs of spine-chilling horror. Their stories awakened a passion within me, and I realized that the genre of horror held a special place in my heart.

Writing allows me to transcend the boundaries of reality, to transcend the limitations of the world we inhabit. It is a gateway to infinite possibilities, where dreams become tangible and thoughts take flight on the wings of words. Through my writing, I strive to share this love for imagination and learning, to inspire others to embrace the power of storytelling and to explore the boundless depths of their own imagination.